The Lost Locket

The Lost Locket

Carol Matas

illustrations by
Susan Gardos

Scholastic Canada Ltd.
Toronto New York London Auckland Sydney
Mexico City New Delhi Hong Kong Buenos Aires

Scholastic Canada Ltd.
604 King Street West, Toronto, Ontario M5V 1E1, Canada

Scholastic Inc.
557 Broadway, New York, NY 10012, USA

Scholastic Australia Pty Limited
PO Box 579, Gosford, NSW 2250, Australia

Scholastic New Zealand Limited
Private Bag 94407, Botany, Manukau 2163, New Zealand

Scholastic Children's Books
Euston House, 24 Eversholt Street, London NW1 1DB, UK

www.scholastic.ca

Library and Archives Canada Cataloguing in Publication
Matas, Carol, 1949-, author
The lost locket / Carol Matas ; illustrations by Susan Gardos.
ISBN 978-1-4431-2865-0 (pbk.)
I. Gardos, Susan, illustrator II. Title.
PS8576.A7994L6 2014   jC813'.54   C2013-905344-1

Cover photograph copyright © Fotosearch.com

6 5 4 3 2 1   Printed in Canada 121   14 15 16 17 18

MIX
Paper from
responsible sources
FSC
www.fsc.org   FSC® C004071

For my cousin Manny, best friend
and for Anna and Sylvia

The author would like to thank editor Diane Kerner for her support. Also thanks to Donna Babcock for the typing of the manuscript. And finally, to Dov Blank who loved the story and never stopped asking, "When will it be published?"

Contents

Chapter 1

The Locket

It all started when my mother placed the small, square, blue velvet jewellery box on the kitchen table. She motioned me to sit down beside her. Then she picked up the box and opened it slowly. She gave me a meaningful look.

I realized that there had to be something awfully important in the box. Mom had even waited till Ben was in bed so we could be alone.

Slowly she lifted out a thin, gold chain. Dangling on the bottom of the chain was a locket. It was shaped like a heart, with a tiny diamond in its centre. She pushed against the bottom of the locket and it opened. She handed the locket to me. Inside were two tiny heart-shaped pictures.

"That's your great-grandmother," Mom said, pointing to a nice looking woman with a little smile on her face and long, curly brown hair, "and that's your great-grandfather." He looked stern.

I shut the locket and looked at it. The gold gleamed and the diamond sparkled.

"You don't remember your great-grandmother because she died before you were born," Mom said. "But today is her birthday. Baba gave me this locket on this date when I was eight, just the same age as you are now.

"Do you think you're old enough to take good care of this, Sarah Rose?" Mom asked.

She'd said my whole entire name. This had to be a very important moment.

"Yes!" I answered.

"All right," said Mom, "it's yours." She paused. "Don't lose it. And if I were you I wouldn't take it to school. It'll get lost there for sure."

I put the locket on the shelf above my bed, thinking it would look perfect with my white and pink dress.

I got ready for bed. I laid out my clothes for the next day at school. 'Course the locket would also look perfect with my green sweater, I thought. I was going to wear that and my black pants the next day. But my mother did say not to wear it to school. . . .

"Sarah, didn't I tell you not to wear that to school?"

It was breakfast the next day, and I was wearing the locket with my green and black outfit. It looked great.

"Mom," I said, trying not to get mad, "I'm not a baby. I won't lose it. Honestly. I just want to show it to everyone."

She sighed.

I started thinking about all the games I could use the locket for at school. Like pretending it had magical powers. Or that there was a secret map inside it. Or — like in the book I'd been reading the night before — you spin it and suddenly you're in another dimension.

"Don't worry, Mom," I said, trying to sound very grown up. "You must trust me."

She sighed again. She shook her head.

"Let me see, let me see," squeaked my baby brother, Ben.

He made a grab for the locket. He's four. Right at that moment his fingers were covered in peanut butter. Come to think of it, they usually are.

"Ben!" I yelled. "Don't ever touch this." I threw on my jacket, grabbed my lunch and kissed my mother. "See you after school," I said.

"Don't forget I'm picking you up!" she shouted after me as I ran out the door. "We have some shopping to do."

"Okay," I yelled back.

Thank goodness I don't have to walk Ben to school. He goes in the afternoon so Mom takes him there and picks him up too.

After the bell rang and we had all hung up our jackets, Sam was the first one to notice the locket. (Sam is short for Samantha, and she's my best friend.) She sort of ogled my locket. Ogle is a word I'd read the night before. That's what the kids in the book did when they met an alien in another dimension. It means you stare so hard your eyes practically pop out of your head.

Soon half the class was oohing and aahing. Carefully I pulled the locket over my head and took it off so Sam could get a really good look.

"Gym!" shouted Mrs. Lester.

I figured I'd better not wear the locket to gym so I put it neatly away in the corner of my desk.

We had a really busy day and I guess I kind of forgot about putting my locket back on.

Anyway, just before the last bell, I remembered. Good thing too. Imagine what my mother would say if I went home without it! I opened my desk and reached for it.

It was gone. Gone! I threw everything out of my desk but the locket was nowhere to be found! I felt like I was in an elevator, going down very fast. I couldn't believe what had happened.

The bell rang. I looked around to tell Sam, but she'd already left. I threw everything back into the desk. I felt sick. For a minute I just stood there not knowing what to do. I knew I couldn't stay in the classroom any longer — Mom would ask me why I was late. So I put on my jacket and started out to the car. I prayed she wouldn't notice 'cause if she did I was dead!

Chapter 2

It's Lost!

"It's not fair," I protested. We were in a grocery store. Mom had picked us up from school and taken us there to buy groceries for supper. I was in a terrible mood after what had happened with the locket, and now Ben was making it even worse. It was the last straw.

"Why isn't it fair?" my mother asked. "You have a handful of candy, Ben has a handful of candy."

"But his cost twenty-five cents and mine cost ten cents," I objected, my voice getting higher and louder. I pointed to the prices written on the candy machines.

My mother sighed. She gave me another dime. I put it in the machine and got another handful of SweeTarts.

"You still owe me a nickel," I said. "It's still not fair."

She gave me a look. "All right," she said, "perhaps we should talk about the fifty cents you get every Thursday when you go swimming."

I hate it when she says smart things like that.

Ben looked at my two handfuls of SweeTarts and his one handful of jelly beans. He started to grumble.

"That's not fair. Sarah got more than me."

My mother opened the door of the store and started out to the parking lot.

"Coming?" she said, and she looked like she'd just as soon leave us both there.

We followed her out. She grabbed Ben's hand.

As we settled into the car, I prayed she wouldn't ask me the question she's asked me every day since I started kindergarten.

"How was school today, Sarah?" she asked, once we were buckled up and driving home. Well, I mean, why should she pick this one day not to ask it? That would be improbable. Meaning, according to my mother, very unlikely.

I didn't reply, of course. How could I tell her that the locket, the very same locket I swore to her I was old enough to take good care of, had disappeared from my desk?

My mother repeated the question. "How was school, Sarah?"

At this point Ben hit me. Of course I hit him back. He started to cry.

"Sawa hit me. Sawa hit me."

"Sarah Rose, you're the big one, you know better than to hit him. He'll never learn to stop hitting if you keep doing that."

"But he started it!" I yelled.

"Benjamin," she said, "don't hit."

He wouldn't stop crying, the brat. He just about kills me, then he cries, and I get yelled at!

Life before Ben, I thought. I'll bet it was great. If only I could remember more about the four years before he was born. They were probably the best four years of my life.

This year, Mom announced Ben would be going to nursery school at Brock. *My* school. At least I'd always been able to escape him when I went to school. I mean, all the nursery schools in Winnipeg to choose from, and she chooses the one at Brock!

It's a nightmare. His classroom is just down the hall from mine, and as soon as school started in the fall, he got this weird idea that he could come and see me any time. The teachers told him he couldn't. But I don't think he believed them. I think he thought they were teasing him.

So I'll be sitting at my desk working, and then suddenly Ben will be at the door, calling for me. I mean, doesn't his teacher watch those kids? He seems to come and go from that classroom whenever he feels like it.

It's so embarrassing! I thought I'd die the first time he did it. All the kids in the class laughed and said how cute he was.

He's got curly blond hair and blue eyes. I have

straight black hair and brown eyes. Everyone thinks he's adorable. But they don't have to live with him. They don't have to come second to him in everything at home.

After we got home from the grocery store that day, the day I lost the locket, I ran straight up to my room and changed into a T-shirt. I was hoping Mom would think I took off the locket when I took off my sweater. The whole time we were in the store, I'd managed to keep my jacket done up.

Mom looked at me when I came downstairs. "You were so cold you kept your jacket done up in the store and now you want to go outside like that? It's not summer yet. Put on your jacket."

She hadn't noticed! I sighed with relief.

I went out to ride my bike before supper. It occurred to me that maybe I should keep riding forever, and never go back home. It would be easier than telling my mother about the locket. What was I going to do?

Chapter 3

Karate Class

At suppertime I only ate one hamburger, three potatoes, some corn and a bowl of salad. So my mom got that worried look I really hate.

"Sarah, is anything the matter?" she said as she passed the potatoes to Dad.

"No," I answered, maybe a bit too loudly. "Why?"

"Because you've hardly eaten."

She was serious, too. All the kids at school tease me about the lunches I bring every day.

"Hey, Sarah," Curtis the Horrible yelled once,

"why don't you just rent a truck to carry that lunch bag of yours to school?"

I can never think of anything smart to answer back to Curtis when he says dumb stuff like that. At least, not until I get home. Then I think of lots of answers. Like, "Well, Curtis, you certainly wouldn't need a truck to carry your brain, it's sooo small." Stuff like that.

Of course, Curtis isn't really stupid, just mean. And I wouldn't have dared say anything to his face because he'd have beaten me up — even though I was as tall as he was. I still am. We're the two biggest kids in the class. I've always wondered why he doesn't eat as much as I do.

Anyway, I can't help it if I'm always hungry. Once I tried not to eat as much, but I almost died of starvation. And I'm not fat — not at all — I'm practically skinny. Mom says I'm just growing fast and I'll slow down in a few years and then I won't be so hungry all the time.

"Nothing is wrong," I repeated to Mom with feeling, hoping she would believe me. "Can I be excused?"

"Yes," she said. "Get your jacket, we'd better get going."

"Yeah," piped up Dad, "off you go, I'll clean up."

"Go?" I said. "Where?"

"Sarah," my mother sighed, "it's Monday night."

Monday night. Monday night. Oh, no — karate. I'd completely forgotten.

"Oooh, do I have to?"

"Yes," said Mom and she started to glare at me and I could feel Dad's glare too. "Now don't start up again."

I had begged them to enrol me in karate this year, so they did. Then I found out that I was the biggest klutz in the world. I wanted to quit but they wouldn't let me.

"You can quit after this year," Dad had said. "But in this family when we start something, we finish it."

So I was forced to go till the end of the year. And it was a two-hour class. My mom took it with me and she just loved it. She was always practising — surprising us from behind doors and shouting and stuff.

I dragged myself out to the car and off we went.

When we got there, the teacher said we were going to learn throws. First we had to do all our exercises. Then we started on the throws. He needed a volunteer.

I tried to hide behind my mother. Mr. Sun loves to use me as a volunteer, I don't know why.

"Sarah," he said, and my heart sank. "Come up to the mat please."

I stepped out from behind Mom — how had he seen me, did he have X-ray eyes? — and walked as slowly as possible to the mat in the middle of the room.

"Sarah, just try to punch me," he ordered.

I racked my brain for a good excuse to get out of this. Like, "I'm sorry, Mr. Sun, but I'm going to faint." Or, "I'm sorry, Mr. Sun, but I'm going to throw up," or "I'm sorry, Mr. Sun, but I'm against violence of any sort." I didn't say anything, though. Instead I took a deep breath, made a fist and tried to hit him in the face.

Wham!

Suddenly I was on my back on the mat. He had grabbed my wrist and flipped me over.

Well, that was lots of fun. I staggered to my feet.

"Now you try." He smiled.

He went to hit me. I grabbed his wrist, turned around and pulled. Nothing. I pulled again. Nothing.

"Now I will show everyone step by step." So slowly, step by step, he showed everyone how to flip. Finally he let me go back to Mom, and she and I practised. She flipped me ten times. I almost flipped her once. Sort of. I mean I was pretty close.

"Don't worry, Sarah," she said, "you'll get it next time. You almost have it. You just need more confidence."

She always says that to me. But where do you get confidence? Can't just buy it in a store, can you?

I was hungry when we got home. I ate a cold hamburger, an apple, an orange and a banana. Then my mom made me go to bed. I don't know why. I'm never tired at night but she makes me go to bed anyway. I think I should wait until I'm really tired, but she and Dad are always fussing at me about getting lots of sleep.

As I lay in bed the whole business with the locket came back to me. I guess one good thing about karate was that it made me forget all about the locket.

The locket.

Oh boy, how would I ever sleep when all I could think about was that?

Chapter 4

We're Detectives!

"I have to talk to you," I whispered to Sam as I slipped into my seat the next morning. We were supposed to be getting ready for French.

"I can't talk to you, or play with you," said Sam. "You didn't bring your lion puppet and I told you to."

I hate it when Sam does that. Everything always has to be her way. She loves to boss me around.

I narrowed my eyes and took a good long look around the room. Somewhere in this room, I thought, lurks a crook. Lurks. That's a great word, isn't it? I read it in this mystery book and used my dictionary to find out what it meant. I have a dictionary this year. Everyone in grade three does. But I didn't understand what the dictionary said so I asked my mom. She said it was sort of like being somewhere, but hidden, and you knew someone was up to no good if they were lurking.

Somewhere in this room lurked a crook.

"You have to help me," I whispered to Sam, who usually sits beside me. "Someone stole my locket."

"Really?" said Sam.

"No," I answered, "I'm just kidding."

"Well, you shouldn't kid about stuff like that," she said.

"I'm not kidding," I replied.

"But you said you were," she answered.

"But I was kidding when I said that," I said.

"What?" she said.

"I was kidding when I said I was kidding," I explained.

"You were kidding when you said you were

kidding, but you really aren't kidding?" asked Sam.

"Are you kidding?" I asked. "I can't follow you."

"No, I'm not kidding," she said. "You are."

Boy, I could hardly remember what I asked her in the first place.

Oh yeah, my locket, that's what I was asking her about.

"I've lost every necklace I've ever worn but I promised I was old enough not to lose this one! Maybe it was stolen. I know I left it in my desk yesterday and when I went to get it at three-thirty, it was gone."

"Do you think one of the kids took it?" asked Sam.

"What do you think?" I asked back.

"Is everyone ready for French?" called Mrs. Lester. "Come along now, children. Sarah, Sam, you don't even have your books out."

"Maybe I should tell Mrs. Lester," I whispered to Sam.

"Yeah," Sam whispered back, "you should. But she's going to tell your mom."

We got into line.

"I'll have to tell Mom, anyway," I went on in a low voice. "But maybe I can wait a day. Maybe we can get it back. Wanna be a detective?"

"Me?" said Sam. Sam is scared of everything. She still sleeps with her light on. It's funny that someone so bossy should be such a scaredy-cat. "We won't have to go into any dark places, by ourselves, at night, will we?"

"No," I answered. "It must be someone from here who took it. We just have to keep our eyes and ears open. *Wide*."

"Okay," said Sam. "We'll be detectives. What'll our names be?"

"Umm," I thought for a moment, "let's see." And I searched my brain for some good names from all those books I'd read. "How about Dynamic Detectives, Dahlia and Dove?"

"Dove," said Sam. "Dove is dumb. Dahlia is nice. I'll be Dahlia."

"No," I objected, "I want to be Dahlia."

"Then I won't play," said Sam.

Once we got to French class we had to stop

talking. I like our French teacher. He always makes us laugh.

"I'll be Rose. It's part of my own name," I whispered. "Then we're both flowers."

"Okay," she agreed.

"Now all we have to figure out is where to start."

Chapter 5

Making Plans

It was early in May and the snow had just finished melting. The schoolyard was full of big puddles. Since March, Mom had been complaining about the weather.

Normally, I wouldn't have cared. I love winter because I go skating all the time. But since April it had been getting warm, then cold, then warm again, so the ice on the rinks was all melted and yucky. It was boring not being able to skate. Then finally we were able to put away our boots and get into sneakers and jackets, and I could ride my bike. But Mom still made me keep my hood up when I left the house for school. I never put it up at recess, though. I didn't want everyone laughing at me.

So it was recess and it was pretty windy and I was thinking that maybe I should put my hood up even though I'd look silly. Sam had hers up. She didn't care what the other kids said.

"Are we detectives now?" she asked.

"Of course, Dahlia," I answered.

"So what do we do, Rose?" she continued.

"Well," I answered, not quite sure myself, "I guess we have to spy on everyone. We have to follow everyone around and see if they're wearing the locket."

It was sort of exciting. Just like in my mystery books.

"Okay," she said.

I put my hands behind my back and began to stroll around the schoolyard. Curtis and Brian had found the biggest puddle in the yard. They were jumping in it. What a mess. Their feet and pants were soaking wet. Mrs. Lester was going

to be mad. She was going to say, "This is not a kindergarten class, we do not keep extra clothes for those who get wet in water play." But then she'd go find them extra socks from the Lost and Found so they wouldn't catch cold. She's too nice to them. They deserve to have wet feet all day if they jump in puddles. But she can't help it. That's just the way she is.

Sam and I circled the schoolyard, staring at everyone in our class. But they all had jackets on and we couldn't see anything. Maybe this wasn't such a great plan. It certainly wasn't working out the way it did in my books.

"You know," Sam said, coming up to me, "this wasn't such a great plan. I'll think of the next one." She loves to be the boss.

"Okay," I said, "you think of a better one."

"I will!" she said.

"Well?" I pressed.

"I'm thinking," she replied.

"Well?" I said again.

"I'm still thinking," she answered.

The bell rang.

"I'll have a plan by lunchtime," Sam declared.

"Okay, lunch," I said.

I can walk home from school at noon, but I like to stay for lunch. Sam stays and we play together. At home I'd be really bored and I'd have to see Ben. He trails around after me and won't leave me alone and drives me crazy.

I didn't care what Sam said — I hadn't given up on my plan. I looked closely at everyone in our class. No luck. At lunch I looked closely at everyone again. No luck.

I guess the person who stole the locket wouldn't be stupid enough to wear it, I thought to myself. They'd be more likely to hide it. Of course. We'd have to look around the classroom. Maybe it was hidden there.

Sam was sitting next to me, eating a peanut butter and jam sandwich (yuck). I was eating corned beef on rye with a dill pickle and mustard, and juice, and two cookies, and some taco chips, and strawberries, and a banana.

Sam said, her mouth all sticky so she could hardly talk (double yuck), "I have a plan. We

28

have to look in the classroom."

"I just thought the same thing," I said, speaking as fast as I could. I can't afford to do too much talking at lunch. I have a lot of food to eat. I concentrate very hard on getting finished.

"Great minds think alike," she said. "But I don't want to do it."

"Yeah," I said, my mouth full of chips, "it's dangerous. What if Mrs. Lester catches us? She could think we're the crooks."

"Yeah," said Sam, "let's forget it."

"No," I said, gobbling up my fruit and Sam's apple core (what a waste, I always tell her), "we have to try. Come on. We'll look around when we go get our jackets after lunch. After all, maybe the locket just dropped out of my desk and someone picked it up, or it's still on the floor or something."

"Well, okay," Sam agreed. "If it's just to look around a bit."

I slowed down with my eating so the other kids would get outside before we did. Then we went to the classroom for our jackets. No one was around.

You don't realize how much junk everyone keeps in a classroom until you start looking for something. We found wads of bubble gum stuck in a corner, half-eaten erasers, pencils, empty Twizzler packages and Skittles wrappers on the floor, books and notebooks everywhere — but no locket.

"Should we look in everyone's desk and tote tray?" I whispered to Sam. Our desks can't hold all our stuff, so we each have a basket, called a tote tray, for our extra things.

"No!" she exclaimed.

"Well, I don't want to, either," I said, "but we are detectives and we should leave no stone unturned."

"What does that mean?" Sam asked.

"It means we should try everything," I answered. "Except maybe looking in people's desks and tote trays. We'd better think about that some more."

"Yeah," Sam said, "let's think outside."

Just then Ben and my mother appeared at the door.

"I have an appointment downtown, Sarah. Will you watch Ben until the bell rings?"

I nodded, my heart pounding in my chest. Suddenly I knew why detectives' hearts always pound in their chests.

Mom stood still and looked at me.

"Why aren't you girls outside with everyone else? Won't you get in trouble for being here?"

Ben grabbed me by my jacket.

"I wanna go on the climber." He dragged me out of the classroom past my mom.

I let him. I sort of shrugged and smiled at Mom She gave us a strange look, as if she was thinking, I wonder what they've been up to.

Thank goodness for Ben, I thought. Then I couldn't believe I'd thought it. I was probably losing my marbles due to all the stress.

Anyway, we had to think of another plan.

Fast.

Chapter 6

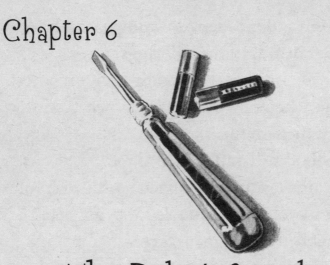

The Robot Speaks

After school that day I went to Hebrew school. I sort of like it. I'm learning Hebrew and about what the Jewish people did in the olden days. I always walk with David, who's also in my class at regular school. We go twice a week. David is okay but he only wants to play robots and stuff. Which is also okay but not *all the time.*

"Hey," I said to him, "want to be a spy?" I was thinking that maybe he'd seen something or maybe he would help Sam and me look for the locket.

"Sure," David replied. "My name is Mechanis Mechanico and I'm a robot spy from the planet Spyaticus." And he started walking like a robot.

"Okay," I sighed. (No use trying to get him to be a person.) "I'm Rose and I'm on the lookout for a super-valuable gold magical locket that has great power. Anyone owning such a locket would have enough power to rule the universe!"

"I will rule the universe," said David in a monotone. "I will own the gold locket. Where is it?"

"I don't know!" I exclaimed. "That's what we have to find out!"

"Simple," said David. "We use our X-ray vision to see through the universe until we find it."

"I don't think we have to search the entire universe," I said. "I think maybe, uh, our classroom at Brock should be good enough."

"I have already seen such a thing in the classroom at Brock School," David announced.

"You've what?" I exclaimed. "You've seen it? Where?"

"I do not remember," he continued in his monotone. "My memory banks must need recharging.

Must need recharging. Must need recharging."

"Yeah, but think!" I said.

"I can't think, my batteries are running out, out, out." Then he stopped as if frozen and pretended he couldn't move.

I opened a pretend panel on his back and put some pretend batteries into it.

"Good as new," I said. "I've put in fresh batteries."

"Thank you," he said, once again moving like a robot. "I will not forget this."

"No, really, David," I urged, "did you really see a gold locket? Because I really lost one yesterday. Remember, the one I was showing everyone yesterday morning?"

"Yes," said David, still being a robot, "I saw it. But where? Where did I see it? Please check my memory circuits. Are they working?"

I pretended to open him up again, this time his head, and take a look.

"No, they're all scrambled up," I said.

"Fix them," he said. "Maybe then I will remember."

I pretended to fool around with tools on the back of his head.

"There," I said, trying not to get annoyed, "all fixed. Now do you remember?"

"No," he said. "That is to say, yes."

"Which?" I said. "No or yes?"

"Both," he said.

"Both no and yes?" I asked.

"Yes," he said.

"Yes, you remember?" I questioned.

"No," he said.

"No, you forget?" I said.

"Yes," he said.

"Yes what?" I screamed in frustration.

"Yes, no, I forget where, but yes, I remember it."

Oh boy, isn't that right where we started?

"But you must remember," I said, ready to bop him. "Try harder."

"I am trying too hard," he protested. "My circuits are beginning to overheat. I am going to blow up. KABOOM." He pretended to explode and threw himself all over the place.

"Did you lose a locket, really?" he said, as he dusted himself off.

"Yes," I replied, "really, and my mom is going to kill me. It was from my great-grandmother."

"That's too bad," David said. "I really did see a beautiful gold locket yesterday. I wish I could remember . . . someone had it in the lunchroom . . . oh yeah, I think it was Curtis."

"Curtis!" I exclaimed. "Oh no, not Curtis!" Why did it have to be the meanest kid in class?

But how did he get it? Did he steal it or just find it on the floor? And what was I going to do about it? Could I just go up to him and ask him if he had found it? Maybe, if I did that, he'd give it right back. Or maybe he'd pretend he didn't know what I was talking about, and he'd hide it and I'd never see it again. I sighed. I was in a real mess.

"You don't look too good," said David to me as we walked up the steps to Hebrew school.

"I don't feel so good," I answered. "Will you keep an eye out for me?" I asked. "If you see Curtis with the locket will you tell me?"

"Sure," David agreed. "You should tell Mrs. Lester," he suggested. "She could ask Curtis for it back."

We walked into our classroom and sat down at our desks. I imagined going right up to Curtis and demanding the locket back. Then I imagined what it would feel like to get hit by Curtis. I imagined my mother asking me where the locket was, maybe asking me to wear it. Trouble is, I could imagine everything except what to say to her.

It was a mess all right. A real mess. A real conundrum. What a great word that is. It means problem. And I certainly had a big one. A great big conundrum.

Chapter 7

What Do You Do With a Bully?

I'm the oldest, right? But do I get to go to sleep latest? Oh no. In fact Ben goes to bed at the same time I do and he's four years younger than me. Four. Now is that fair?

And I can't have sweets after supper because too much sugar makes *Ben* wild. Is that fair? And try to get two words out at suppertime. Ben starts to sing at the top of his lungs and I start to shout at him and Mom starts to shout at both of us and Dad tries to pretend he's in Hawaii and it ends up I never do finish saying what I started to say. Is that fair?

That same day, that is, the night of that same day, I tried to ask Mom and Dad a question at suppertime.

"What would you do," I said, "if this big bully—" Ben started to sing, "— if this big bully," I continued, screaming as loud as I could, "had something that was yours? SHUT UP, BEN!"

Ben kept right on singing.

"Ben," said my mother, "Sarah is trying to talk. Please be quiet and wait your turn. You can sing to us when she's finished."

But Ben continued to sing — if that's what you can call it. Really, he just repeats the same thing over and over again at the top of his lungs. That night he was singing Bully.

"But this is a bully song," he objected, putting that hurt look on.

"I know, honey," said Mom, "and it's a lovely song but we'll hear it after Sarah finishes. What was the question again, Sarah?"

I sighed. "If a bully —"

Ben started again.

"Bully, bully, bully, bully." There was no tune, of course.

"Ben," said my mother, "if you can't be quiet you'll have to leave the table and go up to your room. Wait until Sarah is finished, then we'll listen."

Of course he wouldn't wait. He just kept yelling, "Bully, bully."

Mom got up to pick him out of his chair. Finally he stopped.

"Thank you," said Mom. "Now, Sarah, what was it?"

"If a bully had something that was yours, what would you do?"

"Well," said Mom, "I would go up to him and ask him for it."

"What if he says he doesn't have it but you know he does?"

"I would say I know he has it and I want it back," Mom answered.

"What if he hits you?" I went on.

"Sarah," said Dad, "you know we don't believe

in violence as a solution to any problem. It's always better to talk. But if someone hit me, I'd hit him back. Then he'd think twice before he hit me again."

"But I can't hit him," I objected. "He'll kill me!"

The truth is I was scared stiff of Curtis. I hated the rough games he played at recess and I hated the thought of getting hurt.

"How about a karate flip?" suggested Mom.

"Oh, sure." I laughed. "Fat chance."

"What about your karate defence moves? I'll bet you could stop a punch now," said Mom.

"Nah," I grunted.

"Well," she stated, "I believe in the direct approach. Ask him. Who knows, maybe he'll be very nice about it. Maybe he doesn't even know this thing is yours. By the way," she continued, "what is it of yours that this bully has?"

"BULLY, BULLY, BULLY," Ben started up again.

Mom sighed.

"All right, Ben, your turn."

We all had to listen to him scream for the

rest of supper. But I was very relieved. At least I didn't have to answer Mom's question. What would I have said? "Oh it's nothing, Mom, just great-grandmother's locket that you told me not to lose."

That night, before I fell asleep, I lay in bed listening to music and tried to figure out a plan.

Should I just walk up to Curtis and demand the locket back? No, he'd pretend he didn't have it.

Should I tell Mrs. Lester? No, then for sure he'd pretend not to have it.

I'd have to catch him with it. I just hoped he hadn't sold it or anything. That was something I wouldn't put past him. I'd have to get Sam and David to help me. One of us would have to watch Curtis at all times. And one of us would have to check his tote tray. I just didn't want that to be me. He'd kill me if he caught me.

Karate or not, I didn't want to get into a fight with Curtis. I'm too young to die, I thought. Way too young.

Just then my mother stuck her head in the door.

"Sarah, Baba has invited us to dinner at her house Friday night," she said. "Be sure to wear your locket. She'll be so happy to see that I've passed it on to you!"

"Sure, Mom," I croaked, barely able to get the words out.

" 'Night, dear."

" 'Night."

Well, disaster had struck! I'd have to get the locket off Curtis or face my mother and my grandmother! What a choice!

Chapter 8

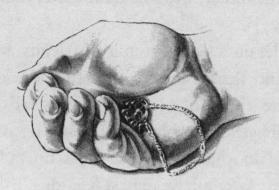

A Rotten Recess

The first thing we did at school the next morning was math. I used to hate math but Mrs. Lester makes it fun and this year I've been getting much better grades.

A small group of us sat around a table with Mrs. Lester while the other kids worked at their desks. And guess who ended up sitting right beside me? Curtis. Now, you'd think Curtis, being the jerk he is, would also be a stupid jerk. But the weird thing is, he's smart. Especially in math.

Anyway, what I can't understand is, if Curtis

is so smart, why isn't he smart enough to know that bullies don't have friends and everyone hates them?

Well, he does have a couple of friends, I guess: Mark and Rudy. They're the stupidest kids in class and they do just what Curtis tells them to do. That's not what I call being friends. Of course, I do what Sam wants me to do, but that's different. After all, we're best friends.

I glanced over at Curtis. He sure looked big. He's much heavier than I am. He has a big head and lots of brown hair which falls all over. He wasn't wearing the locket. But then, why would he? A boy wouldn't wear a girl's locket.

So why did he steal it if he didn't want to wear it? Maybe he did just find it. What if, I thought, I just ask him how he got it? That couldn't hurt, could it? I'd do it at recess. For sure.

"Sarah," Mrs. Lester asked, "are you with us today? You seem to be in a world of your own."

I giggled. I giggle a lot. I can't help it.

"I'm here, Mrs. Lester," I said. Curtis snickered. The morning seemed to drag on and on and on. Finally the recess bell rang, and I told Sam my plan on the way out to the playground. "I'll just go right up to him and ask him," I declared. "And you'll come with me."

"Do I have to?" she said.

"You want me to go alone?" I asked.

"I don't want you to go alone," said Sam. "But I don't want you to take me with you, either."

"Aren't you my friend?" I demanded.

"You wouldn't ask a friend to get into trouble, would you?" she replied.

That was a hard one to answer. Sometimes Sam is just too smart.

"No," I said at last. "I wouldn't ask a friend, a friend wouldn't need to be asked. A friend would just want to do it."

Sam sighed. She couldn't think of a good excuse for that one.

We started over to where Curtis, Mark and Rudy were playing superheroes. Curtis was screaming an order, his arms in the air, his voice loud. In his hand he held a shiny gold object.

"With the power vested in me by this treasure I command you to bow before me," he yelled.

The boys bowed.

"Now, go slay the dragon of DunLevy, and bring me back his wings."

Mark and Rudy drew their swords and charged off down the playground to get the dragon.

Actually it looked like a really neat game. I wouldn't have minded playing.

"Sarah," said Sam, "look at what he's holding in his hand!"

I moved in closer. The treasure was none other than my locket. My locket! I ran up to Curtis, forgetting to be afraid.

"Curtis, Curtis, that's my locket! Give it here!"

Curtis lowered his arm and looked at the locket. Then he looked at me.

"Prove it," he said.

I was flabbergasted. (A word used a lot in spooky novels — people are always flabbergasted when they see a ghost or something — it means they can't believe their eyes, or in this case, their ears.)

For a moment I didn't speak. He was standing there with his hands on his hips, looking like he'd love a fight.

"It's my locket," I repeated, "and I want it back. If you need proof, open it up. There are pictures of my great-grandparents inside."

Instead of opening it up, he slipped it into his jacket pocket.

"Finders keepers."

"You give that back, Curtis," I said, "or I'll tell Mrs. Lester."

"If you do," he said, "I'll tell her I had it, but I lost it."

"You wouldn't!" I exclaimed.

"I would," he declared. "And you couldn't prove it's not true."

"Yes I could, we'll have you searched!" I shouted.

"Then I'll throw it away somewhere you'll never find it!" he shouted back.

"You're rotten, Curtis!" I screamed. "You won't get away with this!"

"Oh yes, I will," he laughed. "Maybe I'll give it

back to you when I'm finished playing with it —
if you're lucky."

"Why I'll . . . I'll . . . " I felt like I could kill
him. But I was also afraid I was going to burst
out crying.

Just then the bell rang.

"You'll what?" He snickered again and pushed
me as he ran past me toward the classroom.

I stood there, in the middle of the playground,
not knowing what to do. And feeling awful.
Could he get away with it?

At that moment everything in life seemed
pretty unfair. And the prospect of having to tell
my mom the whole story was getting too close
for comfort. What a disaster!

Chapter 9

Ben, Curtis, Karate and Me

"Come on," said Sam, "we'll be late. Don't just stand there."

"I can't believe anyone could be so rotten," I said, stamping my foot in anger. "Can you?"

"Yes," said Sam, "if it's Curtis. Come on."

She grabbed my arm and pulled me along.

Mrs. Lester was talking as we walked into the classroom.

"Hurry and take off your jackets, girls," she said. "We'll be working on our science projects this afternoon."

Sam and I went to the back of the class where there are open closets. I put my jacket on a hook. Then I noticed that Curtis's jacket was hanging a few hooks over. All I'd have to do was reach my hand in and grab my locket.

I looked around. Curtis was staring at me. So what? I could still do it, and he'd be too late to stop me.

"Hurry up, girls, right now," Mrs. Lester said.

Rats. She was staring right at me. I'd have to wait till later.

Sam and I hurried over to the supply corner and got all our junk. We were making a model of the solar system out of papier mâché. We coloured the planets, and put rings around the ones that needed rings, and connected everything with wire. I was glad we were doing the project together because it gave us a chance to talk.

David came over and sat down with us for a minute.

"I saw all that," he remarked. "Bad."

"Yeah," I agreed, "but what can I do about it?"

"There has to be something," he said, "just think."

He gave me an encouraging smile, then left to work on his own project.

"He's right," I said to Sam, "we have to think."

"You should tell Mrs. Lester," said Sam.

"And then Curtis would throw the locket away so I'll never find it," I answered.

"How could he do that here, in the class?" Sam asked.

"Good point," I replied. "Maybe he couldn't. Maybe I should tell Mrs. Lester. But what if Curtis threw the locket out the window or something? He'd be in trouble anyway. A little more trouble wouldn't matter. And he'd want to get back at me for telling. So he probably would throw it out the window and it'd land in a very deep mud puddle and I'd never find it again. Or it would break, and how would I explain that to my mom?"

I stopped to think.

"There must be a way," I said, "there must be." Suddenly it dawned on me.

"It's simple. I just have to walk over to the jackets when no one is looking, stick my hand in his jacket pocket and take the locket out."

"He'll see you. You'll never get away with it," Sam said. "He'll run over and grab his jacket."

"We need a diversion," I said.

"A what?" asked Sam.

"A diversion. A big commotion that attracts everyone's attention so they aren't looking at you."

Just then Ben came bursting into the room.

"Oh no," I groaned. "Not again."

"Yeah," sighed Sam, "now there's a commotion."

"Sam!" I exclaimed, "of course!"

Ben was running around the room looking for me, calling, "Sawa, Sawa."

Mrs. Lester just ignored him. She always expects me to take him back to his room.

But this time I decided I wouldn't take him right back to his room. No, this time I had a better idea.

"Ben, we're over here," I called.

He saw me and ran over.

"Ben," I said, "you have to stay in your nursery class. Mrs. Browning is going to worry about you."

"I wanted to see you," he said. "I was lonely."

Mom says he loves me more than anyone in the world. But does he have to be such a pest about it?

"Ben," I said, "want to know a secret?"

"Yes," he said, his eyes shining.

"Do you know who Curtis is?" I asked him.

"No," he answered, shaking his head, his big blue eyes looking up into mine.

"He's that kid over there," I whispered, "wearing the army shirt and pants."

"G.I. Joe?" asked Ben.

"Yeah," I replied. "And G.I. Joe has jelly beans in all his pockets and he told me if you came to class you could climb on him and tickle him and try to get the candies."

"Really?" said Ben, his eyes opening very wide.

For a minute I thought that maybe I was being rotten, but I quickly shook off that thought. After all, I needed my locket back, no matter what.

"Yes, really," I said. "Go on, get them now."

Curtis was sitting on the floor at the far end of the room. Ben ran over and jumped on him yelling, "Candy, candy."

I headed for the jackets. I heard Curtis yelling, "Get off me. Get off me, you stupid baby."

I found Curtis's jacket, and I put my hand in one pocket. It was filled with junk. How was I going to find the locket in that mess?

"Ben, Ben," Mrs. Lester called, "come down off Curtis, Ben. Someone is going to get hurt. Sarah, where are you?"

I put my other hand in Curtis's other pocket. I could feel old jelly beans, nails, candy wrappers, but I couldn't feel my locket.

"Sarah! What are you doing?" Mrs. Lester was looking straight at me. "Please help us with your brother."

Curtis was struggling to his feet. I ran over to him just in time to see him shake Ben to the floor. Ben landed with a crash and started to cry. Mrs. Lester put her arms around him.

"Curtis, that was not necessary," she said in a very mad voice.

I ran over to Ben.

"Are you all right?" I asked him, kneeling on the floor.

He was bawling his head off.

"You, you, you told me," he said, his big blue eyes accusing me. Then he started to cry so hard he couldn't talk. He must have bumped himself when he fell.

"There, there," Mrs. Lester said, "you'll soon be fine, Ben. Now let's go back to Mrs. Browning and we'll check to see if there are any bruises or cuts." She took his hand and led him out of the room.

I went back to the corner Sam was sitting in.

Sam looked at me.

"Well?" she asked.

I shook my head.

"Nothing," I said.

I sat down. I felt pretty bad. No locket, and well, I felt sorry I'd done that to Ben. He did what I told him because he trusted me.

I guess he does love me, I thought. But I don't give him much love back.

And then I looked up to see Curtis coming toward me, his face all mad.

"Hey," he yelled, "you keep your dumb brother off me."

I started to get up. Sam put a hand on my arm. "Don't, Sarah," she warned.

I shook her hand off and got up.

"Don't call my brother dumb," I said.

"Okay," said Curtis. "He's not dumb, he's an idiot. And a dolt. And a nerd. That better?"

"Just like you?" I answered back.

"Why, you . . . " Curtis yelled, and went to punch me.

Well, I guess that karate class did teach me something because suddenly it was like everything was happening in slow motion. I saw his fist coming toward my face. I moved my arm up and I blocked the punch, grabbed his arm, turned and heaved with all my might — and flipped him onto his back!

The whole class cheered, even Mark and Rudy. Just then Mrs. Lester walked back in.

"What is going on here?" she exclaimed.

Curtis scrambled up. It almost looked like he was going to cry.

"Nothing," he muttered, and hurried back to his project.

"Sarah?" she asked.

"Nothing, Mrs. Lester," I said.

"Everyone, back to work," she ordered.

I went up to her.

"How is Ben?" I asked.

"He's fine, Sarah, but please try to talk to him about staying in his room."

"I will, Mrs. Lester, I promise. Thanks." I went back to Sam and sank down to the floor. I felt sort of shaky. I couldn't believe what had just happened.

Curtis was looking at me nervously from the other end of the room.

"Are you crazy?" said Sam. "He could have killed you."

"Well, he didn't," I answered. "And if I hadn't done something he *would* have killed me."

Then I looked at her.

"And while I think of it — I don't like the way

you boss me around all the time. You shouldn't make the rules about what toy I have to bring, that's not fair."

Sam stared at me. Boy, was she surprised.

"Yeah," she said, "I guess you're right. I'll try not to do it any more."

Wow! It was my turn to be surprised. I never figured sticking up for myself would be so easy. I felt a lot better. I'd stood up for Ben and for myself.

But I still didn't have my locket.

Chapter 10

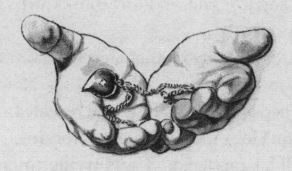

Learning a Lesson

"Sarah," Mom said to me at suppertime, "what is this story about Ben getting hurt in your classroom today?"

My heart sank.

"Oh that," I said.

"Yes," she said. "That. But what is that? Ben says you told him Curtis had candies for him, and then Curtis hurt him."

I was in a real fix, that's for sure. I didn't know what to do. Just blab the whole story out and get it over with? Or try to stall for just a bit longer until I could think of something that would get me out of this jam? I tried to stall.

"I'm sorry," I said, "I didn't think Curtis would hurt him."

"But, Sarah," my mother objected, "you've told me many times what a bully Curtis is. Now, what happened exactly? Exactly," she repeated.

It didn't look like stalling was working.

"Well," I muttered, "I was trying to create a diversion."

"A diversion?" questioned Dad. "Why?"

"Well," I said even more softly, "I wanted to do something without Curtis seeing me do it, and that's why I told Ben to go over to him and tickle him."

"You used Ben," said Mom in a very quiet voice.

I nodded my head.

"Curtis hurted me," Ben declared, looking like he was going to cry again.

"Sorry, Ben," I muttered. "I didn't think, really, about what would happen to you."

"Well, I'm not sure sorry is good enough," said Mom. "What do you think?" she asked Dad.

"I'd like to know what was so important she was willing to sacrifice her own brother," said Dad.

Things were getting worse and worse.

"Well, I didn't think of it like that," I stalled.

"No," Mom remarked, "you didn't think, did you?"

Oh boy, I was really in trouble. I was definitely in more trouble than if I'd told them I'd lost the locket in the first place. Because then I'd only have been in trouble for losing it, not for losing it and not telling them and getting Ben hurt.

"Well," I said, "remember great-grandmother's locket?" I felt sick. Positively sick. Maybe I'd faint and I wouldn't have to tell them. They'd be so worried they would forget all about the whole thing.

"Yes?" they replied together.

"Locket, locket, locket," Ben started to sing. "Just a minute!" He got up from the table and ran upstairs.

"Where are you going?" called Dad.

But Ben didn't answer. He never does.

"Well . . . " I started, wondering how I could put this so it wouldn't sound so bad. There didn't seem to be a way. I stopped.

"Yes?" Mom said. "Go on."

"Okay," I said, and I took a deep breath. I felt like someone standing in front of a firing squad. "I took the locket off," I said, talking really fast to get it over with, "and put it in my desk and really it was safe, Mom, but Curtis stole it. Or found it," I added. "I'm not sure which. And then he wouldn't give it back. But I knew he'd put it in his jacket pocket so I told Ben to look for candy on him and I went to check out Curtis's pockets but I couldn't find the locket."

"What do you mean, he wouldn't give it back?" said Dad.

"Just what I said. He wouldn't. He said he'd throw it away if I told Mrs. Lester."

"Don't you think you should have told us?" Mom demanded.

"Yeah," I said, "but he never would have admitted it to a grown-up."

66

"Still," said Dad, "what you did to Ben was wrong."

"It wasn't fair," Mom said.

"No," I agreed, making a face, feeling like I was going to cry, "I guess it wasn't."

Well, this was it. The absolute pits. That means the bottom. Rock bottom. And I'd hit it. My parents knew I'd lied. They were looking at me with that disappointed look that's worse than yelling. I'd hurt Ben, and I still didn't have the locket. My only consolation, the only thing that made me feel better, was the thought that things couldn't get any worse.

"Well, I'll just have to phone Curtis's parents," Mom said, getting up from her chair. "Then he'll have to give the locket back."

Okay. I was wrong. Things could get worse!

"No!" I almost screamed. "No! You can't! Curtis will deny it and then he'll throw the locket away so we can't prove he took it and we'll never find it and then he'll come to school and go after me again. Although," I added, "he doesn't scare me any more!"

"Well then, Sarah," Mom said, folding her arms, "if I don't phone his parents what would you suggest? If you can't think of anything else, I will certainly phone."

I mashed my vegetables around with my fork. But I couldn't come up with one idea, even though I was racking my brain. I could feel the tears starting to burn my eyes.

Just then Ben came running into the kitchen. He climbed into his chair. His fist was all clenched up. He put it in my face.

"Don't," I said, getting peeved with him again.

He opened his hand.

A small gold locket lay in his palm.

I stared at it. I couldn't believe my eyes.

"My locket! Ben, where did you get my locket?"

"In Curtis's pocket," said Ben. "You told me he had candy for me. But he got mad at me and pushed me. He was bad. You should always use words when you're mad."

I reached for the locket.

"Mine," he protested. He closed his fist over it.

"Ben," said Mom, "it is Sarah's locket."

"Just a minute," I said.

I ran up to my room and threw things around on my desk until I found a small brown bag. I ran downstairs and sat down again at the table.

"Trade?" I said to Ben.

"What?" he asked.

I took out a big chocolate egg all wrapped in gold. Sam had given it to me at Easter. I'd been saving it.

Ben's eyes lit up.

"Trade," he said.

He handed me the locket.

I actually felt like kissing him. I never kiss him. But I did. I kissed him.

"YUCK," he yelled, wiping his cheek. "I hate kisses."

I clutched the locket happily.

"Let's go play," I said to Ben.

"Together?" he said, hardly believing his ears.

"Yeah," I said. "Together."

I guess things didn't turn out too badly after all. Curtis shakes like a leaf every time I come near him and he never bullies anyone — I just have to give him a look and he backs off. Sam doesn't boss me around any more, either. And I wouldn't say Ben is my best friend in the world — he still basically drives me crazy — but a part of me actually likes him now.

Mom and Dad forgave me, but not until I'd had a very long lecture about honesty being the best policy. Which is true. But sometimes you just have to handle things yourself. And now I know I can!

As for my locket, I only wear it on special occasions. The rest of the time, it stays safe and sound in my jewellery box. And Baba was very happy to see it on me at dinner that Friday night!

About the Author

Carol Matas didn't always want to be a writer — she started out as an actor and began to write while expecting her first child. Now she is the author of more than two dozen best-selling books for young readers, including *Daniel's Story* and the Dear Canada books *Footsteps in the Snow, Turned Away* and *Pieces of the Past.*

Carol's books have won many honours, including the Silver Birch Award and the Red Maple Award. She lives in Winnipeg, Manitoba.

Maleficium

Also by Martine Desjardins

Fairy Ring
All That Glitters
A Covenant of Salt

All available from Talonbooks

MALEFICIUM

Martine Desjardins

Translated by Fred A. Reed and David Homel

Talonbooks

Talonbooks
P.O. Box 2076, Vancouver, British Columbia, Canada V6B 3S3
www.talonbooks.com

Typeset in Arno and printed and bound in Canada.
Printed on 50% post-consumer recycled paper.
Typeset by Typesmith.

First printing: 2012

The publisher gratefully acknowledges the financial support of the Canada
Council for the Arts, the Government of Canada through the Canada Book
Fund and the Province of British Columbia through the British Columbia
Arts Council and the Book Publishing Tax Credit for our publishing
activities.

Maleficium by Martine Desjardins was first published in French in 2009 by
Éditions Alto. We acknowledge the financial support of the Government
of Canada, through the National Translation Program for Book Publishing,
for our publishing activities.

Library and Archives Canada Cataloguing in Publication

Desjardins, Martine, 1957–
[Maleficium. English]
      Maleficium / Martine Desjardins ; translated by Fred A. Reed and
David Homel.

Translation of: Maleficium.
ISBN 978-0-88922-680-7

      I. Homel, David II. Reed, Fred A., 1939–
III. Title. IV. Title: Maleficium. English.

PS8557.E78284M3413 2012   C843'.54   C2011-908717-0

For Michèle Mayrand,

who waited for this book a dozen years,

and for my niece Béatrice

untouched by slimy toads

!
●

CAUTIONARY NOTE
TO THE READER

IT HAS LONG BEEN RUMORED that the Archdiocese of Montreal held a book so dangerous that it had been consigned under lock and key to the most inaccessible reaches of its secret archives. Whoever might presume to exhume it from oblivion would be excommunicated forthwith and could entertain no hope of absolution. The archbishop himself systematically denied the existence of such a book of the damned: the scandalously notorious *Maleficium* by Vicar Jérôme Savoie. While the substance of this work has long remained a mystery, numerous self-proclaimed authorities have come forward to vaunt it as a heretical treatise or an exorcist's handbook – so much conjecture, based on little more than rumor and speculation.

Little is known of the life of Vicar Savoie (1877–1913). Born into a market gardening family from Côte-des-Neiges, he completed his studies at the Grand Seminaire, took Holy Orders at age twenty, soon after became vicar of Saint Antoine parish and ended his days assigned to a monastery after having been struck by a sudden and inexplicable attack of deafness. The recent discovery of eight sealed folios among the priest's correspondence with one of his nephews gave rise, among collectors of ecclesiastical arcana, to hope and disbelief in equal measure. Several expressed doubt that the cramped, nearly illegible handwriting revealed on these ink-smudged pages could possibly be that of Jérôme Savoie. Exhaustive research, however, has made it possible for us to authenticate the manuscript, and to confirm that what had been discovered was indeed the text of *Maleficium* in its original version.

This, the first edition, presented here in substantially revised but unexpurgated form, is certain to cause discomfort, and perhaps even disapprobation. For Vicar Savoie's work consists of transcriptions of confessions heard under the seal of the Holy Sacrament, thus breaking the bonds of the oath he had sworn to uphold, and which neither law, nor threat, nor peril of death could force him to reveal. In a note in the margin justifying his decision to violate the most sacred of all trusts, he asserts that he possessed the deepest and most absolute conviction that he had become the victim of a malevolent force, and that the salvation of his soul, and that of the Church itself, lay in the balance. We can well understand why the staff of the archdiocese did everything in their power to ensure that these shocking revelations never saw the light of day.

The highest ecclesiastical authorities have already attempted, using whatever influence they could muster, to impede the propagation of Vicar Savoie's work, going so far as to threaten anyone associated with its publication. There is every reason to fear that, by opening *Maleficium*, the reader will be exposed not only to the stain of these depraved confessions, but may well risk excommunication. You have been warned.

THE PUBLISHER

STIGMA DIABOLICUM

TWO YEARS HAVE PASSED since my last confession. At the time, my face was still intact; I had not yet been forced to adopt the leather prosthesis I now wear in place of a nose. I know, Father, that we must accept the trials that heaven visits upon us, though I cannot but avow the bitterest rancor regarding my infirmity. You would understand why were I to tell you that I was employed as a spice buyer by a well-known Bombay importer and that, having lost my sense of smell, I was forced to abandon my trade. Upon my return from India, a few months ago, I opened a shop close by Jacques Cartier Square where I sell premium-quality spices – that, at least, is what my sign proclaims, in carmine lettering on a gold-leaf background. But, to tell the truth, I could not swear whether the cardamom, nutmeg and cinnamon I sell my customers is fresh or stale. I do, however, guarantee the excellence of my saffron. My stock includes varieties from Spain, Kashmir and Iran, the only three places in the world where *Crocus sativus*, the violet flower that produces the world's most costly aromatic substance, is cultivated.

The aromatic and coloring properties of saffron are concentrated in the three short endings of its pistil, known as a stigma, through which pollen penetrates the plant to fertilize it. There are unscrupulous merchants who try to pass off a mixture containing the base of the pistil, and even the stamen. I stock only *mongra* – pure, first-quality saffron. You have the reputation, Father, as a gourmet, and I have even heard that, on occasion, you slip on an apron and prepare daring *pièces montées* and complex *chauds-froids* that never fail to impress the select circle of your guests. It is said that your specialty is a saffron-syrup savarin. Given the discriminating power of your palate, you are well placed to appreciate, more than any other citizen of our city, these few pinches of saffron I harvested myself in Srinagar. Search from one end of Kashmir to the other, you could find none quite so rare, for it lends a reddish, and not a yellow, hue to any food it touches. Bring your face closer to the confessional screen and breathe in its scent. Do not be repelled by the astringent vapors that flow from it; smell it as if you were about to devour it ... There! Already it is too late to turn away, you are staggering, you feel your senses are about to take leave. If, suddenly, I were to pull it away from beneath your nose, you would be hard-pressed to contain your anger; the tone of your voice would rise by several notes. Does the aroma of these crimson threads, as it worms its way into you, not awaken venomous thoughts in which the dolorous sweetness of depravation melds with the joyful bitterness of corruption? Though I cannot smell it, I experience fleeting visions of opening boddices, contagious lips, insistent thighs. I feel myself wallow in the depths of the most culpable reveries ... I would not sell it for any price. Put yourself in my place, Father; these strands of saffron cost me my nose! Allow me to tell you how this misfortune occurred.

It is unlikely I would ever have set foot in Kashmir had I not been forced to leave Zanzibar. There I busied myself negotiating agreements with local clove planters, supervising the harvest and overseeing the packing of the merchandise, which I would then ship to Bombay before the monsoons came, where my associate, Nadir Bandra, would sell it to incense manufacturers and Javanese cigarette makers. Nadir could command a price four times greater than I had paid, which provided us with a substantial profit of which I took thirty percent. Of course, our margin depended on the market price of cloves, but our business was prospering. You may know, Father, that the clove is not a seed, but the bud of a flowering tree. The bud is harvested just before flowering, when it begins to turn red. Its peduncle is removed and dried on large racks until it acquires the hardness of wood. Since the buds are delicate, the operation must be carried out with the greatest care, and it is so fastidious that Zanzibar workers view it as a demeaning task. They seek the slightest pretext – famine, epidemic, blood feuds between clans, a new superstition – to decamp. One day, a rumor was started that a succubus was haunting the warehouse, chasing after men, better to flog them with its long tail. No doubt this vicious rumor was started by one of my rivals, but which one? In Zanzibar, the competition between clove exporters is fierce, and I had made many enemies. The workers were terrified and refused to return to their jobs. By the end of the week, the entire year's harvest had been ruined by mold, and with no hope of recouping my investment, I had to resign myself to closing the business. All that remained was to tell my partner the bad news. I packed my bags and took passage on one of those teak-hulled corvettes that crisscross the Indian Ocean. As we were leaving the port, I cast a last, regret-filled gaze upon the swaying palm trees and the red-tinged clove plantations that lined the hillsides. There I stood until the island on which I had lived the past seven years of my life was no more than a nebulous blur on the horizon, illuminated by the rays of the setting sun.

In Bombay, Nadir welcomed me with open arms, and seemed singularly undistressed by the turn of events. He had for some time been thinking of launching a more lucrative business, he confided, and he had a new venture to propose to me. But the details would have to wait until after dinner, when his spouse would prepare *paan* – a confection of lime mixed with grated betel nut, anise seeds and cardamom with just a touch of powdered porphyry to stimulate virility. Seeing her spread the mixture on a silvery betel leaf, then form it into a roll that she held together with a clove, I grasped why the Indians consider the preparation of *paan* as the most graceful task to which a lady's hand might lend itself. As I chewed the invigorating substance, whose only drawback is that it leaves one's mouth stained red, my host revealed that he intended to enter the saffron trade.

"Do you know," he said, "that this aromatic substance is currently worth more than gold?"

That was more than enough to convince me. When my partner added that saffron was particularly abundant in the Srinagar region, I volunteered to leave for Kashmir without delay, there to conclude supply agreements with producers and obtain the fruit of their next harvest. Nadir welcomed my proposal enthusiastically, warned me against the various ruses employed by Srinagar merchants and advanced me the where-withal required to commence operations.

Early next morning, I departed as the smoke from the night's fires still hung over the streets of Bombay. The station was already thronged. On the platform, submerged by a human tide, I was assaulted by porters' cries and the screaming of a thousand babies. Travelers called to me, offering a piece of halvah or a handful of roasted chickpeas. By some curious paradox, in a land where food is rare, people are quick to share – particularly in times of hunger – while in our countries, where abundance reigns, we jealously set aside our provisions.

Nobility can truly thrive only where there is adversity; the rest of the time, man is all too content to look after his own pleasures, happily enough, I might add, for traders like myself.

I traveled first to Delhi, and then on to Simla, from which I would proceed to Jammu. There, I learned the railway line went no farther, and if I wished to reach Srinagar, I would have to find a wagon to transport me. As luck would have it, I met a family making its way to the valley on a pilgrimage, and they offered to take me with them. These pilgrims were not Hindus off to worship the great ice lingam in the Cave of Amarnath. No, they were British people by the name of Sheridan, and they hoped to receive the blessing of a mystic woman living at the Christian mission in Srinagar. During the journey, which proved quite lengthy because the wagon kept getting stuck, the paterfamilias asked where I was from, if I were married, if I played polo – the kind of questions that ostensibly seek information, but reveal more about the interests and concerns of the questioner. I feared I might appear diminished if I answered, so I offered a few laconic responses, and the conversation soon lapsed. I was relieved when the wagon emerged from the forest of deodars and onto the broad avenue lined with plane trees that led to the city. I took leave of the Sheridan family at the mission door and struck out in search of lodgings.

The Maharajah Pratap Singh, who ruled over Srinagar, was an eccentric who enjoyed playing cricket in gold-embroidered slippers. Untrusting by nature, particularly with regard to colonials, the prince had forbidden the British from owning property in the valley. The British elite, which traveled north to the cool shores of Dal Lake during the monsoons, had floating dwellings built, creating a summer retreat all the more agreeable in their eyes since they were removed from the Moslem populace. Several of these residences were for rent, and I took up quarters in a spacious vessel that contained, along with the kitchen and servants' quarters, two bedrooms and a bathroom, as well as a paneled study with a veranda that overlooked the lake. At sunset I was regaled by the spectacle of purple martins come to feed from the great bronze platter of its tranquil surface as the muezzin's sad call expired. The following morning, when I awakened, the lake had turned turquoise, and carp fishermen were already casting their nets. I breakfasted on a cup of sugary tea and some fruit, then hurried off to the bazaar. The entrances to the market were obstructed by yaks laden with silk, with those famous shawls that had brought fame to Kashmir when the Empress Josephine ordered four hundred for her personal use. The stalls overflowed with varnished papier-mâché bowls, walnut-wood utensils, and urns and jars overflowing with rice and lentils, ghee and dried apricots. Women clad entirely in black kneaded bread while their husbands in striped caftans smoked patchouli in water pipes or chewed on lotus stems – in scrupulous respect of local usage that requires one to touch food only with the fingertips of the right hand. An old man thrust a prayer mat into my hands and, to demonstrate that it was made of silk, ripped off a strand and lit it. The strand flared like a black-powder fuse and sparked into nothingness; had it been wool, it would have burned slowly. Once I rid myself of the unwelcome fellow, I made my way through the smoke of roasting chestnuts and, guided by my infallible sense of smell, located the aisle of the spice merchants. As far as the eye could see lay pyramids of cinnamon, cardamom, cumin, turmeric and finely stone-ground red pepper.

In Zanzibar, I always considered myself an extremely skilled bargainer. But the rapacious merchants of Kashmir quickly put an end to such pretense. They remained inflexible on price, and were not disposed to offer me the slightest advantage. Nadir Bandra had not exaggerated when he described their mendacious business practices: to a man, these consummate thieves attempted to sell me saffron mixed with silk fibers, distaff thistle flowers or shreds of pomegranate. I was forced to make the rounds of the entire bazaar before finally coming upon an honest saffron broker. This plump, affable man, who hailed from the nearby village of Pampore, was prepared to consign to me his entire harvest at a reasonable price. Though it would take him several days to deliver the crop, he offered me a pound of the saffron he had in stock as a token of good will. What he showed me appeared to be of good quality. I decided to trust him and the deal was concluded.

As I was returning to my lakeside refuge, I encountered Sheridan, the patriarch of the pilgrim family. He dismounted his pony to shake my hand – an effusiveness I found startling, considering the coldness with which we had parted. He was overflowing with praise for the mystic at the mission, a young woman of such humility that she drank the very water with which she washed the feet of lepers. He had heard that each day she visited a monument known as the Roza Bal and, wishing to follow in her footsteps, had decided to visit the place as well. He asked me to accompany him.

"It's quite close by," he said, as if to reassure me. "In the Khanyar district."

The Roza Bal, he explained as he took my elbow, was the mausoleum of Yuz Asaf, the prophet venerated in Ahmadiyya Islam. Its adherents held that Yuz Asaf was none other than Jesus Christ, who had survived the torment of the crucifixion and, to escape his persecutors, had come to live out his life in Kashmir, where his enlightened preaching had won him the title Leader of the Healed. As mausoleums go, Roza Bal was far from extraordinary; hardly bigger than a house, built of rammed earth, it had green-shuttered windows and a terraced roof. The entrance nestled beneath an archway and opened onto an antechamber that led to the sanctuary. We should have removed our shoes, but since the place was deserted, we did not bother and strode without a second thought across the sacred carpets. In the middle of the sanctuary stood a tall, rectangular enclosure of finely wrought wood whose detail was hard to appreciate in the dimness. Inside this sepulchre lay the prophet's sarcophagus – a worm-eaten box set atop a base and draped with a threadbare orange cloth. Perhaps my visit to the spice market had disturbed my sense of smell, but it seemed that a powerful odor of saffron pervaded the place. Yet no one had placed offerings of any kind before the tomb. We rapidly made the rounds of the shrine; Sheridan, visibly disappointed, announced that he had seen enough.

"In any event," he added, pulling out his watch, "it's time to return to the mission. Today is Friday, and the young mystic will receive stigmata at three o'clock. It is said to be something sublime and transcendent to behold. Would you like to attend?"

I politely declined the invitation. Aside from the fact that I had no desire to see a self-styled communicant bleed, I wanted to be alone in the sanctuary and seek out the source of the smell of saffron. Once my companion had withdrawn, I toured the funeral chamber once more, this time paying closer attention. I lifted the carpets and stirred the dust in the darkest corners, but found no hint that might explain the origin of the troubling perfume. Could it be that the smell came from the sarcophagus itself? I pressed my nose against the finely worked wooden screen, but was unable to discern anything. Having brought nothing to light my way, I resigned myself to abandoning the search. "In any case, there's probably nothing inside," I said aloud in the resonance of the room.

I spoke too soon. From the depths of the sepulchre, a voice responded, a voice that caused the blood to run cold in my veins, so sudden and unexpected was its sound. How could I describe it to you? It spoke in a whisper, breathily, with sinister inflections that reminded me of the hissing of a serpent.

"And I," the voice replied, "am I nothing?"

I heard a match strike, and light spread through the inside of the cage.

I put on my most threatening tone and demanded, "Who goes there?"

The only answer was the opening of a small door that blended in with the grillwork surrounding the sarcophagus. I took a careful step forward, then another, and bent over cautiously. How great was my astonishment when I discovered, in the depths of the sepulchre, the frail form of a young girl in a squatting position, who was holding a candle at arm's length. She could have been no more than seventeen. She was dressed in a missionary's tunic, with a rosary knotted around her waist; a white shawl framed her face and a long veil covered her body from head to foot. In the flickering candlelight, her skin was the color of wax and the whites of her eyes looked yellow, which did not diminish the perfect innocence of her features. However, the angelic simplicity of her smile was broken by an unsightly cleft in her upper lip. She suffered from what is commonly known as harelip.

"Are you the mystic from the mission?" I asked.

She nodded, and beckoned me to draw closer. How could I resist her call? The scent of saffron grew ever more intoxicating as I approached. I entered the sepulchre on my knees and discovered, in front of the tomb, what the girl wanted to show me. It was a block the size of a paving stone into which two footprints, each pierced by a narrow hole, had been imprinted.

"Look," she whispered, pointing to the two perforations. "Nail marks."

The mystic was convinced that these impressions represented the feet of Christ, and the holes, the place of the stigmata. I objected, pointing out that the marks were not symmetrical, and were certainly the result of natural forces. She would not be dissuaded, and went on in her hissing voice.

"That is easily explained. When the Romans crucified people, they used only one nail to pierce the two feet, one atop the other."

As if to demonstrate, she removed her sandals and climbed atop the stone, left foot above her right. She must not have cut her toenails in years, for they resembled claws. For a moment she sought her balance, then, eyes closed, hands crossed upon her chest, she spoke in a low voice.

"The asymmetry of the stigmata is the irrefutable proof that Christ is buried here. If he were never resurrected, that would mean he is not the Son of God. Which means that his place at the right hand of God is free!"

I was shocked by what I heard. Did the mystic hope one day to take that place? Her face seemed so transfigured by ecstasy that I would not have been surprised. As she continued to mouth other equally blasphemous utterances, my eye was drawn to the top of her feet, where her sandal straps had left red marks that corresponded exactly to the holes of the footprints. Her veins were swollen at that spot, and throbbing wildly. Before I could warn the mystic, her taut and finely textured skin parted like the peel of an overripe fruit, and from the furrows of her exposed flesh a fluid oozed, so bright red it verged on yellow. I was about to stanch it with my handkerchief, but something stayed me. The odor of saffron that pervaded the air in the cage was overpowering, and I had to draw my own conclusions: it was coming from the incisions of the girl with the stigmata. But I had no time to investigate further, for she chose that moment to faint in my arms. I laid her down on the carpets of the sanctuary and did my best to revive her.

"Take me back to the mission," she implored when she regained consciousness.

As I helped her tie her sandals, I noticed that the hemorrhage had ceased and the smell of saffron dissipated. Had this all been a dream? Not only were her wounds healed, but they had not even left a scar on her feet.

~

Three days later I took delivery of the saffron. I had no reason to linger in Srinagar, and should have departed immediately for Bombay. But I decided to extend my stay until the following Friday to witness the appearance of the stigmata one more time. The mystic had not converted me, far from it. In the course of my previous journeys to India, I had seen a sufficient number of fakirs buried for hours in sand, piercing their flesh with daggers or allowing themselves to be bitten by cobras to no longer believe in miracles. Upon reflection, I decided that the apparition of the stigmata must be a trick. I suspected as well that the blood that flowed from them was fake, and that its strong and particular odor was due to the saffron used as the main coloring agent. I could not accept that someone would employ that noble aromatic substance to deceive honest people. It was my duty to unmask the mystic, hold up her secret for all to see and denounce her hypocrisy.

When I presented myself at the mission, Sheridan answered the door. He told me the girl had received stigmata every day for the last week.

"It is a privilege for us to attend, but she is in such a state of prostration we fear for her health – especially should she bleed again today," he said, casting an uneasy glance toward the shore of the lake where the mystic had withdrawn to meditate before her great effusion.

His naivety was so pathetic that I was strengthened in my resolution to shake the scales from his eyes. I left him at the door to the chapel where the faithful were already praying as they awaited the mystic's arrival. The coast was clear. I slipped down to the shore where I found the girl stretched out in a *shikara*, a kind of canopied gondola. Her feet, as well as her hands and forehead, were tightly bandaged. When I approached, she sat bolt upright with all the vigor of someone in perfect health.

"Man of little faith, what are you doing here?" she asked, as though she had intuited my intentions.

I had nothing to hide: I told her I had discovered her subterfuge and would soon reveal her hoax to the entire mission.

"I'm willing to wager you're concealing several pints of false blood under your tunic, and that you intend to employ it to good effect. My nose never deceives me. Right away I recognized the scent of the saffron you're using as coloring. I could even identify the merchant at the bazaar where you procured it."

"Don't be so thickheaded," the mystic replied. "Nature provides us with a multitude of analogies in form as well as structure. Why must the scent of saffron have only one source? Mine does not derive from the crocus and, if you wish to discover the source, you will have to accompany me to the floating gardens."

I suspected she was playing for time in an attempt to escape the humiliation that awaited her. Still, she had piqued my curiosity. If another plant possessed the same aromatic properties as *Crocus sativus*, was it not in my interest to see for myself? In any event, the false mystic would get what was coming to her. I stepped into her gondola and cast off the mooring rope. The *shikara* is steered by a sort of heart-shaped paddle, and it took me some time to familiarize myself with the helix-like movements needed to propel it. As the gondola veered in one direction, then another, the girl pointed out to me, on the far shore of the lake, the twelve terraces of the Nishat Bagh – the Garden of Pleasure – and, farther on, the gushing fountains of Shalimar Bagh, the most luxuriant of the 666 gardens bequeathed to Kashmir by the Mogul emperors.

"Some people compare Srinagar to Eden," she said. "When I came here, I felt I was close to paradise."

13

I asked her ironically if, in like manner, she caused her stigmata to appear so that she might draw closer to Christ. Her face darkened and her harelip curled with disgust.

"Why would I follow the example of that minor prophet when I can easily surpass him?"

I must admit that her latest blasphemy was more than I could tolerate.

"Better to say nothing than utter such enormities."

"You don't believe me?" the girl hissed. "And yet I have one more stigma than he does! It is my secret one, and the suffering it causes me is simply excruciating."

To show my disapproval I pretended not to have heard, and went on paddling among the water lotus. Inept paddler that I was, it was all I could do to reach the floating gardens, the rafts of reeds on which the gardeners of Dal Lake cultivate melons, vegetables and flowers, too, using manure and lake grasses as fertilizer. I was grateful to finally arrive for my hands, unaccustomed to such exercise, were covered with blisters. I showed them to the false mystic.

"Look, I have stigmata, too!" I mocked her.

It was her turn to ignore my words. To put me in my place, she ordered me to moor the gondola behind a raft of orange carnations. Grumbling, I obeyed. Was she trying to convince me that carnations could replace saffron? She would not deceive me quite so easily.

14

"Who said anything about picking flowers?" she spoke. "I chose this place because the gardeners never come here in the afternoon. We will not be disturbed. For I have decided to show you all."

With a languorous movement, she drew the curtains of the canopy and began to unwrap her bandages. I held my breath. In hopes of learning at last what lay behind her supposed stigmata, I allowed her yet another of her little *mises en scène*. Her eyelids closed, and her features converged on that critical point where the eyebrows meet in a frown of concentration. You would have sworn her face was transformed with the tension caused by great suffering. Despite the close attention I paid to her every movement, she pulled off her trick with such skill that once again she fooled me. The blood flowed now not like a trickle, but an eruption, in thick, impetuous pulsing from the orifices that opened on her feet, her hands and in the form of a crown on her forehead. Soon her tunic was stained red on the left side, just below her heart. The hemorrhage was so spectacular that I was almost alarmed. But I did not allow myself to be distracted. I took the girl's hand and placed my index finger on the incision. My deepest convictions were shattered. My finger, which should have easily wiped away a few drops of artificial blood, penetrated the incision without encountering the slightest resistance, and passed through her hand from one side to the other!

If I cried out, I was too astonished to hear it. Yet even in the face of clear proof, I continued to doubt. To be entirely sure, I needed to plumb the other wounds. You cannot imagine the effort I had to expend to bring my fingers close to those vile openings. My distress was all the greater, for in her wounds, I could sense only the iron odor of blood. Yet the scent of saffron hung heavy beneath the curtained canopy, more intoxicating than the most powerful alcohol, and more elusive as well, for it was impossible to determine its source. My spirit was so tormented that I lost all sense of measure. When I saw the mystic about to enter one of her ecstatic trances, I feared she would slip through my fingers. Driven by the need to pry open her secret, whatever the cost, I shook her mercilessly.

"The smell of saffron, where does it come from?"

Her lips parted and she spoke.

"Beneath my tunic ..."

In a single movement, I lifted her skirt and uncovered her legs, which were streaked with long ribbons of red-orange blood. Suddenly the heady scent of saffron caught in my throat and tears welled in my eyes. There could be no further doubt: the source of my disquiet sprung from the very nature of the girl. Gently, I lowered my face into the space between her thighs and traveled upward until I reached their forks.

Have you ever heard of the *Stigma diabolicum*, Father? Yes, of course. As a theologian, you would not be unfamiliar with the trials of the Inquisition. You are aware that it is a mark the Devil leaves upon his disciples, preferably on their most intimate parts. I am confessing; I shall speak without restraint. The mystic possessed a devil's mark in the center of her corolla: a long, muscled, fleshy horn-shaped pistil of that intense red called crimson. From it, as from a poisoned chalice, bloody clots oozed. First I recoiled from that vile appendage, but I soon succumbed to its venomous odor. I filled my nose, my throat and my lungs with it. I was lost in what I could only describe as olfactory contemplation – a state that quickly consumed my other senses. Overcome with the most burning ecstasy, I experienced exalted visions, tasted forbidden flavors, heard music most profane.

A burning sensation in my nostrils pulled me roughly from my delight. I drew back and found the cool air soothing, but immeasurably insipid. The crimson saffron opened the doors to a pagan world I had hardly begun to explore, in which I wanted to immerse myself once more. Would I have to become a disciple of the mystic and wait, along with the faithful, for those altogether too-rare moments when she received her stigmata? I did not care for that constraint; I needed privileged access to the girl. I glanced in her direction. She lay motionless, still in a trance. I could, of course, seduce her. But, on second thought, what was stopping me from using her unconscious state to take her most precious possession? I acted rapidly, for she was likely to regain consciousness at any moment. Delicately, I spread open her corolla with one hand and, with the other, grasped the pistil at its base. Pulling with all my remaining strength, I broke it off in a single movement. There was a dull snap, but no excessive bleeding. The mystic gave no other sound than a long hiss through her harelip. I drew the curtains of the canopy around her and, wrapping the stigma in my handkerchief, hastened back to the mission. No sooner did I alight on the shore than I fled, without a care for the state of my victim.

I departed Srinagar that very evening, under cover of darkness. In my bags, along with the Pampore saffron, I carried the stigma, already half desiccated. When I reached Jammu I purchased a vial in which to conserve it, and sealed the aperture with wax, satisfied that I had captured its aromatic essence. On the train to Bombay, my nose began to bleed violently. As the bleeding did not last long, I paid little attention. But the condition recurred several times during my journey, and again in my partner's offices, where this time neither pinching it nor inserting gauze tampons stanched the flow. They sent for a physician who examined me, and immediately detected lesions and papules in my nasal cavity. He opined that these were the early symptoms of leprosy. But I knew what had caused the irritation of my mucosa. Particularly since the bleeding now occurred at regular intervals, each afternoon at exactly three o'clock. Like a condemned mystic, I now received the stigmata through my nasal orifices, and my condition grew worse. Anemic, too weak to raise myself from my bed, I had no idea how to halt the abundant loss of blood. After having tried in vain to cauterize my nostrils with red-hot irons, I resolved to fight fire with fire.

In its vial, the stigma glowed red like an ember from the nether regions, dark, yet brighter than flame. I pried open the seal and breathed in its powerful vapors. A sudden dizziness – that was all I felt at first. But the perfume of saffron quickly went to my head, creating a sense of exaltation that resembled delirium and lasted until the next morning. When I came to my senses, the blood had ceased to flow and my nose, as well as the inside of my nostrils, was encrusted with scabs. I thought that I was saved. The illusion was short-lived. For my nostrils, tickled to the depths of the nasal cavity, were suddenly shaken by a series of violent sneezes. So powerful were the spasms that the scabs dropped off one by one, then by the dozen. I brought my hand to my nose. I could not find it! All that remained were two ridges of brittle cartilage that disintegrated the moment I touched them.

I lost my sense of smell. But if I must confess everything, the perfume of saffron, the last thing I breathed in, was imprinted on my memory and, from that day on, has never left me. You, too, Father, must remember it every time you prepare a saffron-spiced savarin. What's this? You're sneezing. I hope you haven't come down with something. Bless you, as the British say.

FLAGELLUM FASCINORUM

FATHER, I ACCUSE MYSELF of failing to provide hospitality to a neighbor last evening. I never attend the theater or the operetta, yet I do not disdain the occasional concert, and I can frequently be seen in the prime seats at Windsor Hall when the day's most eminent artists favor us with a visit. I did attend Paderewski's recital and, afterward, the spectators rushed to reach their carriages, for rain had begun to fall. The shower was gentle compared to the monsoons I experienced in Zanzibar. There, the skies open without warning with a force that can knock you over. The drops sting like lashes and blind you; puddles will swallow you up should you be so unfortunate as to slip and fall. For all that, I had no intention of getting wet, and opened my umbrella. Imagine my indignation when a shameless individual of imposing stature, wearing a top hat to boot, took hold of my sleeve and began walking alongside me. The umbrella, like its antithesis the shower, is a selfish comfort no one should be obliged to share – especially not with an intruder much larger than oneself. I pushed the interloper away, but it was too late: the rain had touched the thick coating of powder that covers my face, forming pasty clumps that stuck to my fingers.

I admit it: my face is more thickly floured than a mime's, as if I were a guest at a masked ball. Coquetry, you say? Think again. I would gladly dispense with my makeup if I still possessed milk-white skin like yours. As a physician, I am well placed to know that we all have our physical imperfections. I should hope for nothing less than to accept my own, let me assure you. Unfortunately, even if I were to do so, I would still appear to be blushing, for my capillaries are clogged by an excess flow of blood. Beneath the powder, my epidermis is streaked with long crimson striations that make me look like a child's candy cane. Shame seems to have colored my skin the way indigo stains the skin of the desert Tuaregs. I cannot present myself to a lady without her suspecting me of coveting her with unseemly thoughts, and undertaking to make me avow sentiments entirely foreign to me. Men imagine that they intimidate me and take pleasure in treating me condescendingly under the pretext of putting me at ease. My embarrassing affection has had a negative effect on my practice, too. Patients, Father, need certainty above all; wandering in the fog of their symptoms, they seek to understand the illness that torments them and the pathway to recovery. They care nothing for the diagnosis of a practitioner whose reddened complexion seems to express hesitation and confusion or, worse yet, inebriation. *Physician, heal thyself*, the Gospel advises us. But I am unable to find a remedy. I have tried everything: bismuth, oak apple, magnesia, arnica, quinine, camphor, Glauber's salt, valerian … without success. Unsurprisingly, since the cause of the malady that afflicts me is deeply rooted in the circumstances that led me to Africa.

Perhaps you made the acquaintance of Sir Edwin Benedict when he was consul in Montreal? No? That's hardly surprising, for he spent precious little time here, and kept his distance from the clerical collar. Had you been so fortunate as to meet him, you would have certainly been impressed by his elegance, his highly developed intelligence and affable manner. Immediately after completing his studies at Balliol College,

Oxford, he entered the diplomatic service and followed Lord Cromer to Egypt, where he remained for many years. His mission to Canada, which bored him excessively, was strictly commercial, and he dreamed only of returning to Africa. I often wondered why, for he was hypochondriac in the extreme. He approached me one day in Dominion Square after having noticed my kit. Lifting the cuff of his trousers to show me a simple bruise, he inquired whether it was on the verge of turning gangrenous. I was fresh out of my residency back then, and had not yet established my clientele. I took the time to examine the consul, prescribed him a drawing ointment and agreed to visit him the following day. He was waiting for me in his bed. His gangrene had disappeared, but now he was suffering from acute encephalitis.

"I must soon depart for Ethiopia," he whispered, "and my health has never been in such a precarious state. I have a proposal for you: would you agree to accompany me as my personal physician?"

The appointments he offered me were generous enough to allow me to purchase a clientele upon my return, and I accepted on the spot.

Portsmouth, Gibraltar, Cairo, Djibouti: those were the way stations on a journey I had precious little opportunity to enjoy, as Sir Edwin demanded I be constantly present at his bedside should he suffer an attack of the croup. In Addis Ababa, despite four false embolisms and innumerable cases of *angina pectoris*, the consul played a significant role in the negotiations leading to the treaty of alliance with Menelik II. I myself was introduced to the Negus who, as you may know, claims direct descent from King Solomon and the Queen of Sheba. Clad in a flowing mantle of brushed velvet that set off his golden tiara, he sat atop a dais, both hands clasping his scepter. When he learned I was a physician, he proudly announced that he himself was a healer. He drew his powers, he explained, from the holy hosts he clipped from the pages of the Bible, and through whose species he received communion. He assured me that in like manner he could thwart the evils that beset his realm. He had recently freed the region of Lalibela of an infestation of insects come from the nether regions – eyeless locusts of livid tint – by ingesting the chapters of Exodus that describe the ten plagues of Egypt.

The ink on the treaty with Menelik was hardly dry when Sir Edwin was summoned to Zanzibar, the clandestine crossroads of the slave trade along the East African coast. The diplomat's mission was to persuade Sultan Hamud to bring it to a definitive end. But the negotiations were cut short when Sir Edwin, having learned that several cases of cholera had been discovered on the island, decided to pack his bags and return to England on the first boat. I had no desire to leave Zanzibar, which had enchanted me from the first time I saw it. The climate was most clement and the clove trees lent their scent to the breeze. The British consul attachés, amiable by nature, would pour me a gin whenever I called at the club. I had made the acquaintance of Sajid Ismail, a charitably minded nabob who had founded a dispensary and was seeking a physician to assume its direction. Eager to deal with true illnesses after having hunted Sir Edwin's chimeras for so long, I was not about to miss such an occasion to put my talents to the test. I took up residence in the villa that Sajid Ismail placed at my disposal – an elaborate pastrywork of festooned balconies and leafy balustrades, with stained-glass windows the color of candied fruit and plaster meringues built ten years earlier to celebrate Queen Victoria's golden jubilee. The dispensary occupied the entire ground floor and consisted of a large waiting room, an examining room and a private surgery separated from the pharmacy by a partition of hand-carved teak. No sooner had I begun my practice than I encountered striking cases of malaria, leprosy and yellow fever, then diphtheria, sleeping sickness and difficult childbirth. All went well, and I never lost a patient. I rapidly acquired a reputation, and an enviable renown among the diplomatic corps. Soon they came from as far afield as Dar es Salaam and Mombasa to consult me. After a year's time, I enjoyed all the advantages of prestige and authority, with a fortune to match. I opened the dispensary only in the morning, reserving my afternoons for house calls to my better-off patients. Of an evening, when I was not invited to Sajid Ismail's residence, I dined at the club, then retired to the library where I read the London papers. On Sundays I strolled along the harbor, watching the dhows make their way out to sea. What more carefree existence could a man wish for?

During the summer of 1899 – the last I would spend in Zanzibar – I had the singular honor of being summoned to the side of Sultan Hamud during one of his bouts of lumbago. I brought him relief with such success that, as a token of his esteem, he presented me with a ruby as large as a quail's egg. I was likewise invited to the annual celebration he gave in the gardens of Beit al-Ajaib – the Palace of Wonders, so named not for its grandiose architecture or its prodigious splendor, but simply because it was equipped with an electric lift. Never had I attended such successful festivities. An orchestra played on the lawn, amidst peacocks with spreading tails and a chattering throng of ladies in colorful silks. In the shade of the teak trees, young servants in white gloves offered rose-water sorbets and petit fours decorated with mimosa blossoms. I was introduced to the German ambassador, to Admiral Rawlins and the vizier of the British Protectorate, Sir Lloyd Mathews, who had come accompanied by his spouse and her protégée. The latter young lady, whose name escaped me, stood in front of the cage where the sultan kept his captive monkeys, throwing them petits fours and giggling as they fought over the crumbs. Shocked by the lack of *savoir vivre* in a person of her station, I felt myself compelled to intervene.

"You should not be doing that," I whispered as I drew close to her. "You might well be insulting our host."

The mischievous young lady's answer was to cast a petit four in my direction. She was by no means a child; she must have been nearly twenty. Rather pretty – pretty enough not to leave a bachelor of my kind indifferent – though her upper lip was split by a congenital deformation, probably a gap in the alveolar ridge. But it was not her face that drew my attention, but the curve of her lower back as she turned away from me, a precipitous plunge that produced a sensation of vertigo, softened by a perfectly sculpted rump that filled out her gown far better than any bustle. As I admired her, I thought of that famous Ingres painting of the odalisque stretched out on a divan, which the critics disparaged because she had three vertebrae too many.

With a slight shrug, the girl pointed out that the sultan had already withdrawn to his harem.

"They say he has a hundred concubines," she murmured from behind her peacock-feather fan, with a slight hiss no doubt caused by her malformation. "Every night he sleeps with five of them – two on each side and one at his feet – chosen by his eunuchs to ensure an equitable rotation among the women. It seems that's the only way to keep peace on the home front."

I found her last remark, spoken with a touch of naughtiness, rather amusing. Tickled by the risqué turn of the conversation, I adapted my reply to the circumstances and whispered in the girl's ear.

"Hardly surprising that he suffers from lumbago."

With a muffled titter she thrust her fan between the bars of the cage and shook it to excite the monkeys that promptly began to shriek from atop their perches. The moment could not have been more propitious for a demonstration of my scientific prowess.

"Those little devils," I said, "are red colobus – a species to be found only in Zanzibar. They can be recognized by their black faces and pink highlights, their white manes and their flame-red backs. They have no opposed thumb. Their tail is twice as long as their body, and ends in a plume that naturalists call a whip."

She released her hand from the cage and turned toward me.

"Since you are so well versed in zoology, Doctor, can you tell me if monkeys also suffer from back pain?"

"I doubt it," I answered, "since it is a punishment native to the vertical position. Man pays a high price for the privilege of standing upright."

"So the sultan would certainly be better off were he to walk around on all fours."

"Indeed," I said. "At our next consultation, I will suggest he become a quadruped."

"Then all he would be missing is a tail to keep the flies away."

No sooner had the girl spoken these words than she put on a serious look. Why, she asked me, did God in his infinite wisdom not consider it appropriate to bestow upon man what he so generously provided to animals?

"The tail is of indisputable usefulness," she continued. "Without one, are we not like a ship without a rudder?"

Not wishing to venture too far onto such terrain, I simply noted that many naturalists claimed our distant ancestors were equipped with tails. My circumspection served only to increase her curiosity.

"Is it true that the human embryo is endowed with a protuberance of sorts that disappears when the legs are formed, but that certain individuals never lose, and keep throughout their lives?"

Her question caught me off guard. I was startled that a young girl would be aware of such a monstrosity that even physicians never discuss among themselves.

"A child may be born with a deformity at the base of the spine," I carefully broached this unpleasant subject. "But it is no more than a sausage-shaped appendage of soft flesh, not a true extension of the spinal column capable of movement. Which demonstrates, in my opinion, that man does not descend from the apes."

"Are you quite certain?" she said in a defiant tone, snapping shut her fan.

Before I could formulate a response, she took leave of me with a gracious curtsy and went to join Lady Mathews, who was waving to her excitedly. As I watched her move away, I could not stop myself from feasting my eyes on her long, graceful back on which the sunlight, filtering through the foliage of the teak trees, fell so flatteringly. For a moment, it seemed that the vertiginous slope of her lower back was no more than an effect of light and shadow on the silk of her gown. But, with the sudden splendor of illumination, another explanation stood before me. With a mixture of stupor and fascination, I suspected that, like the Grande Odalisque of the Ingres painting, Lady Mathews's protégée had, in the sacral region of her spine, three vertebrae too many.

I did not have the chance to see the girl in the weeks following the reception at the sultan's palace. With the summer heat, a fresh cholera epidemic had broken out in several villages in the southern part of the island, and I was charged with taking appropriate sanitary measures. You may know, Father, that cholera is contracted by drinking water contaminated by the *Vibrio cholerae*. This bacillus does not owe its name only to its curved shape. Once it enters the digestive system, it sprouts a tail – the flagellum – that it agitates when it wishes to move and better spread its toxins. It can finish off a grown man in a matter of hours. The best way not to perish from this microbe is not to catch it. Happily, it is possible to avoid contagion by simple hygienic measures, but they are difficult to apply in such primitive circumstances. The villages worst affected by cholera were inhabited by former Wahadimu slaves whose sole means of subsistence is making rope from coconut fiber. Their huts stand in the midst of open-air cesspools filled with stagnant water, where coconut shells are left to macerate for months before their fibers are supple enough to be woven. These filthy cloacae provided the incubator in which flies in their legions would lay their eggs. In veritable clouds they hovered over the villages, dragging their legs through excreta and depositing the disease wherever they alighted. They were so numerous, and their buzzing so deafening, that it was impossible for me to work. By some malicious instinct, they would take to the air just as I went to swat them, and return no sooner than I had driven them away.

Noticing my exasperation, the man acting as my interpreter – an Indian who spoke English as poorly as he spoke Swahili – led me to the outskirts of the village, to a hut we entered without knocking. I collapsed onto the stool he showed me and looked around nervously. There, seated on a woven mat, in front of a cold brazier, an elderly rope maker with blank eyes was busily weaving lengths of coconut fiber. The hut was full of ropes of varying lengths and thicknesses hanging from the flimsy sticks that held up the roof. At least that was what I thought at first glance. But, as my interpreter explained enthusiastically, the man was a maker of fly whisks, and what I had taken for lengths of rope were the tails of animals he had hung to dry. Should I desire one, he added, I need only choose. There were water buffalo and leopard tails, along with those of mongooses, lemurs, bush babies and hyraxes. In the dim hut, I looked with distaste at the boneless, flaccid appendages hanging there. In that village besieged by insects, a fly whisk would have been of no use; instead I needed a real tail … As I went to leave that place with no further ado, my eyes were drawn, amidst the pendants, to a sinuously curved object that awoke in me the shimmering recollection of my encounter in the sultan's gardens. There was a splendid red colobus tail, thin, quite long, with a matted tuft at its extremity. No sooner had I laid hands on it than the old man unleashed a torrent of words in a threatening tone. According to the interpreter, he was warning me that this was a particularly powerful fly whisk.

I purchased it for a few rupees and headed for the village, happily swinging my new weapon through the air, very pleased to see the flies part as I advanced. In any case, my efforts were not the true cause, for during our visit to the elderly craftsman, the wind had changed. Now it blew from the southeast in sudden gusts that swept away the flies and sent them out over the sea. On the horizon, a wall of clouds was closing in on us. The monsoon in all its might was beginning, and its deluge could not be far behind.

A few days later, the cholera epidemic was under control and I was able to return to the town. I was exhausted. Instead of opening the dispensary, I spent an entire week in my room, shutters closed. I had brought back the monkey's tail in my satchel, and laid it on my bed to keep it within reach. Several times a day, I found myself weighing it in my hand, hefting it, examining it. All the while, of course, I felt I was caressing the endless spinal column of Lady Mathews's protégée. I emerged from my apartments the following Sunday, determined to lay eyes on that miracle once again. Though the weather was threatening, I did not bother taking an umbrella, and proceeded to the Anglican cathedral where Sir Lloyd Mathews was in the habit of attending Mass. I sought out his protégée in the assembled congregation, and caught sight of her moving toward her pew. How could I not have recognized her? She was wearing a gown of peacock-blue taffeta whose black piping played gracefully against the rounded perfection of her form. Against all hope, she was alone. I moved to the pew just behind her. You would not think ill of me, Father, were I to confess that on that day I was distracted from my prayers. Each time the girl kneeled, between the rosary of her spine and the medallions of her rump, I could gaze upon the long, admirable cascade of her back. Meanwhile, it became ever harder to hear the sermon, for the rain had begun to fall, drumming on the cathedral roof with ever-growing ardor. Soon its din overcame even the sound of the organ. No sooner had the service ended than the faithful rushed for the exits in their haste to return home. But the girl remained in her pew, imperturbable, and did not even lift her head when I approached her. At the risk of disturbing her in her meditation, I greeted her and reminded her who I was.

"Pardon me for not having recognized you," she said. "I was lost in thought, reflecting upon the suffering this place has witnessed."

I did all I could to reassure her: the cathedral could have seen no more than a limited number of unfortunate souls, given its recent construction. She replied that the choir loft was built upon the site of the former slave market, and the altar situated at the very spot where once had stood the stake to which captives were chained and whipped before being sold at auction.

"The longer the slaves endured the blows, the higher the price they commanded," she said, getting to her feet. "Was their torment not worse than the insignificant flagellation of Christ?"

I am a fervent abolitionist, Father, and nothing is more odious in my eyes than the brutalities of the slave traders. But never would I compare them with the indignities inflicted upon our Lord, and her comment seemed utterly out of place. All the same, I followed the girl to the front steps, where the downpour stopped us from going any farther. So opaque was the rain that it was impossible to see the other side of the street. Lady Mathews's protégée had come on foot, and intended to return that way once the clouds had dissipated.

"I'm afraid you might be here for a while," I warned her. "With the monsoon, the situation can go on like this for some time."

You may well say that the gentlemanly thing to do would have been to leave her in the shelter of the cathedral and find her a coach – but such consideration would have been contrary to the design I had devised, in the meantime, to cast light on the mystery of her spinal column. I suggested that she seek refuge in my quarters, for I lived nearby, promising to escort her myself to the vizier's. With her consent, I offered her my arm and steered her through the ankle-deep puddles.

Just as I had hoped, by the time we reached the dispensary we were soaked to the skin. The girl's gown clung to her skin, sketching out each delicate spinal process of her backbone. With the bad weather, my private office took on a seductive allure with its carpets, pillows and deep, upholstered divan. I went off to find a peignoir and a linen towel and, taking advantage of my physician's authority, recommended that my guest remove her damp clothing as quickly as possible, lest she catch her death. Opening the door to the examination room, I directed her to a screen behind which she could change while I prepared tea. As I was lighting the stove, she appeared in the doorway.

"I cannot manage to unhook my dress," she said, turning her back to me.

That was the chance I had been hoping for, and I grasped it greedily. I had never before grappled with the complexities of women's clothing, and it took me some time to understand the various closures. For all that, my inexperienced fingers accomplished the task without excessive clumsiness, particularly since each fastener released brought with it the reward of another vertebra of that coveted spine: the first six cervical vertebrae, barely perceptible beneath the velvet of her neck, then the seventh, whose protuberance prefigured the voluptuous convexity of the twelve thoracics. I went from ecstasy to delight. In my haste to reach the lumbar arch, I hardly noticed the red striations that marked her skin with troubling regularity. The discovery, in the sacral region, of scars similar to those I had observed on the backs of former slaves slowed my pace. It seemed improbable that those lesions could have been inflicted by a torturer's lash. Their nearly vertical angle indicated they were the result of self-mortification. What possible reason could Lady Mathews's protégée have to whip herself that way?

But I could not pursue my investigation, for the gown opened no further and the girl slipped from my hands. Regretfully, I let her vanish behind the screen. Instead of setting the water to boil, I stood in the corridor, the victim of unwholesome curiosity that had nothing scientific about it. I contrived to build shameful schemes to convince her to let me examine her, study her and most of all touch her to the fullest extent. But before putting my plan into action, I first had to discover if she did indeed possess a hypertrophied sacrum. The drumming rain drowned out the sound of my footfalls. Why not take advantage of the noise to slip into the examining room and there, hidden in the shadows, spy upon my subject through the open work of the screen?

It took me a moment to make out her figure amidst the confusion of skirts and underskirts, blouses and corsets that she had hung about her to dry. She was bent slightly forward, rubbing her legs vigorously with the linen towel, and providing me with an exceptional view of her rear. I had been expecting to admire the volume of her excellent buttocks and the fullness of her generous hips. What I beheld took my breath away. At first I refused to believe my eyes. But I had to admit that Lady Mathews's protégée's spine did not end at her coccyx. It extended for a further seventeen caudal vertebrae, the diameter of which grew progressively smaller. Covered by scaly skin from the base to its sharply pointed extremity, that tail – how else could I describe it, Father? – was not at rest. The girl was striking her flanks with it, displaying all the nonchalance of a languorous lioness. Anyone who has not acquired a certain detachment from the cadaver under dissection in the anatomy theatre might have found such a deformity repugnant. Not I. I fell to my knees at the sight of this fallen angel's appendage that seemed to defy the Creator with all the bravado of overweening pride. As a mouse creeps toward the snake that fascinates it, I extended a furtive hand toward her arrogant ornament, and with temerity touched it. The reaction was quick in coming. Her tail stood upright, and like the crack of a whip, it lashed my right cheek all the way to my chin. So violent was the blow that my head flew to one side and I heard my cervical vertebrae snap.

You will agree that there is no greater humiliation than a blow to the face. When the bishop wants young candidates for confirmation to understand the most grievous outrages a Christian must endure in the name of his faith, does he not slap them on the cheek? The human face, with its twenty-six muscles that can combine in ten thousand distinct expressions, is the mirror of our emotions; if it is slapped, our deepest sense of self is mortified. That is why it is so difficult to turn the other cheek. But I had no difficulty doing so, and did not even blink when I was hit with another blow. I endured more still, I don't know how many, for the simple pleasure of contemplating the sinuous movements of that perfectly articulated tail. For all its extreme agility, the muscles of the appendage must have become atrophied as a result of lengthy inaction, for after a certain time it began to show signs of weakness, and hang between her legs. I wanted to provoke it again, and encourage it to stand upright. I assure you, Father, I was only holding it delicately by the tip. Imagine my surprise when her tail, like a lizard's, fell away from her rump and lay in my hand! I looked at the girl contritely, ready to offer my heartfelt excuses. She did not seem to be suffering at all, and dismissed me casually.

"You may keep it. I shall soon enough grow another."

Still shaken by what had happened, I barely had the strength to retreat into my surgery and lay the tail on the divan, where it whipped back and forth one last time before expiring. Slowly I regained control of my emotions. I stepped to the window and noticed the rain had stopped. The sight of my face in the mirror frightened me. The lashes had left long crimson welts on my cheeks and forehead, very much like the deep scars duelists so proudly display. I applied a small amount of olive-oil pomade, certain that the red marks would soon disappear. When I left my surgery to tell my guest that tea was served, I found the dispensary empty. The girl had used a break in the weather to flee. I felt a keen sense of regret, but found consolation in the fact that I now possessed the tail, which I could scrutinize at leisure with my magnifying glass to understand how it had broken away from her body. The conical muscle tissue easily spread apart, the vessels had contracted to avoid loss of blood and, as for the vertebrae, they presented natural fissures that allowed the column to break off at several points. These observations gave way to other less orthodox suppositions. Was the tail a manifestation of a primitive nature that reappeared after lengthy evolution? Were we to believe that man had descended from an ancient race of reptiles? My mind was open to every aberrant thought. I don't know how far I might have pushed that heresy had a cloud of flies not interrupted my cogitations. The little vermin had slipped through the open windows and now filled my surgery. They were drawn to my person, no doubt attracted by the olive-oil ointment. I tried to get rid of them with a newspaper, then a towel, then a broom, but to no avail. Exasperated, I grabbed the human tail and waved it above my head. The flies dropped by the dozens. I chased them through the surgery, cracking my whip. I finished off those that clung to me by flagellating myself, happy to put an end to such a nuisance.

I withdrew to my apartment to wash. As I removed my clothing, I saw that my skin was covered by red marks wherever the whip had struck. I thought nothing of it, and applied a generous coat of pomade before retiring. When I awoke the following day, the marks had not disappeared. Instead, they had grown darker, almost crimson, and they have not faded since. Shame is written on my face with indelible ink. Shunned by Zanzibar society, abandoned by my acquaintances, I returned home only last month. By day, I remain inside, confined to forced seclusion, avoiding the eyes of those around me. I venture out only by night, and only wearing this clownish makeup ... I have come, Father, to warn you. The girl with the reptilian tail has arrived in our parish; I saw her yesterday. She will come to tempt you, for you, as do I, appreciate the beauty of a female rump. Do not deny it. Just now I saw you watching the ladies leaving the church. Heed my advice: when a girl with a split lip kneels before you, close your eyes before she turns her back to you. If you don't, you may end up red faced.

LARVAE INFERNALES

DO NOT BE OFFENDED, FATHER, by this picnic lunch in my hamper. I fear my confession will be a lengthy one and, since I have very little meat on my bones, I prepared a small snack to bolster my strength. No meat – that goes without saying – for today is Friday. Only a loaf of bread and a slice of fresh muskellunge, whose odor is unlikely to disturb you, as it is irreproachably fresh. I caught it myself this very morning with great effort, as the bugger weighed more than eighty pounds. Ha! A scaly light just flashed across your eyes! I recognize the fever of the man who finds pleasure in dipping his line in search of fish, using the excuse that the basic elements of meditation are to be found in his rowboat. No need to blush, Father. The hunt is off limits for members of the clergy, but you are certainly allowed to fish, especially since four of the twelve apostles plied that trade. Isn't the most moving episode of the New Testament the miraculous draught of fishes in Lake Tiberias? Saint Luke's description of the two boats overflowing with silvery fish never fails to make me take up my rod and creel and head for the river.

I keep my distance from the port, where there is nothing but ordinary perch. I keep going till Longue Pointe, where passing boats do not frighten the fish with their whistles and throbbing propellers. Lately I've had some exceptional luck: pickerel, sturgeon and even a pike that I cooked in pastry and served with clarified butter. Of course my exploits with the rod are not due to luck, but my choice of bait. No artificial flies for me! I raise my own lures in my garden gazebo. For bait, I prepare a mixture of moldy bread, suet and roast chestnuts, tar, honey and coagulated blood, or sometimes the viscera of a cat, saffron and turpentine, which I macerate in a glass jar. You would be impressed by the size of the maggots I raise in a skinned sheep's head hung from the porch roof. I also have a series of compartmented boxes in which I store live insects – grasshoppers, cockchafers, mayflies, bees and plump crickets. Where worms and leeches are concerned, I keep them on a bed of moss that I sprinkle regularly with a decoction of walnut leaves. To make them more active, every day I feed them a spoonful of well-beaten egg yolk mixed with cream and a sprinkling of anise seeds. And I always brush them with ivy oil or veal marrow before attaching them to the hook, which extends their life in the water.

Despite the fact that I have a new reel, the finest weighted Florentine horsehair line and a patented float, never until today has a muskellunge deigned to nibble at my hook. You may well argue that it is impossible to catch a large muskellunge with worms, no matter how they wriggle, and I would not contradict you. This fish – how well I know it – is the devil of the water! Even hungry and desperate, it will turn up its nose at the most appetizing bait, for it is a carnivore whose diet consists of muskrats and ducklings – when it is not busy attacking careless puppies that stray too close to the shore. You sit motionless, Father, hands folded, fingers intertwined, eyes lowered, as though you fear the rest of my confession. Fear not: I did not offer a living puppy as a sacrifice to the Leviathan. I simply discovered a bait no fish can resist: a parasite I contracted last year in Ethiopia, and that I finally rid myself of this very morning!

You may find it hard to believe, considering how frightfully thin I am, but I have always been quite plump. I grew up in my father's bakery, where he fattened me on brioche and warm bread. To this day I have an insatiable appetite for buckwheat, rye or white-flour dough. This appetite led me to my interest in insects that destroy cereal crops. I forgot to mention that I am an eminent entomologist, an elected member of the Royal Society of Canada, the Linnean Society of Ottawa and associate of the Department of Agriculture's experimental farm. I established our country's insect infestation surveillance network. The locust is my preferred subject of study. As you know, these migratory crickets are listed among the plagues God visited upon Egypt to punish Pharaoh for holding the people captive. Locusts travel by the billions, and can strip a field bare in a few bites. Our North American continent has not experienced such a plague since the mysterious disappearance of the Rocky Mountain cricket. It has been forty years since the great cloud covered the entire surface of Wyoming and Colorado. But last year an entomologist found a specimen in southern Manitoba, which sounded the alarm in Ottawa. I was the logical candidate to devise a method for fighting the encroaching Acrididae if ever they were to return. To this end, I was dispatched on a research mission to the Arabian Peninsula, where locust swarms arise.

Crickets are by nature solitary. But a rapid expansion in population density will cause them to suddenly become gregarious. Promiscuity makes them change into locusts: their green bodies turn brown and they form swarms whose behavior is similar to that of clouds, living stratus and cumulus formations driven by the prevailing winds. Having learned that abundant spring rains favor the hatching of locust eggs in the south of Yemen, I took passage for al-Mukalla. When I arrived, I found the port paralyzed. A customs official informed me that, in a matter of weeks, locusts had devoured the country's major resources, including the bushes from which incense is derived, and there was nothing left to export. The devastating swarm had migrated west, in his opinion, and should have reached the Horn of Africa. I did not hesitate; I took a dhow sailing up the Gulf of Aden for Djibouti. From there, accompanied by a guide and porters, I followed the trail through the ravaged coffee and cotton plantations on the high plateaus of Ethiopia, careful to avoid the territory of the Danakil warriors who fashion the virile members of their enemies into bracelets. I moved upstream to the source of the Tekeze River. I was hot on the heels of the swarm; according to the information we were able to glean, it was not more than two days away. I stepped up the pace, forcing the porters to quicken their stride. Then, abruptly, just when we reached Lalibela, we lost all trace of the locusts. The city had suffered a strong earthquake the day before, and the tremor had probably dispersed the swarm. My guide did not agree. He held that Lalibela enjoyed magical protection against insects because it bore the name of its founder, a king of the Zagu dynasty. While still in his cradle, this king had been encircled by a swarm of bees which did him no harm – an irrefutable sign that he was destined to reign. In the Amharic language, Lalibela means "he whom the bees respect." Despite the absurdity of the hypothesis, I had to concede that there was not the slightest fly, mosquito, ant or termite in the entire town.

Not knowing where to go now that I had lost my locust guides, I allowed the porters to set up camp at the city gates while I went off to dine at the only inn in the vicinity. There I made the acquaintance of a Swiss engineer, his wife, their young son and his governess. The engineer, whose name was Alfred Ilg, had come to Ethiopia at the invitation of Menelik II. To test him, the Negus first asked him to make a pair of shoes, then a rifle. Once he had accomplished those two tasks to his satisfaction, the engineer was awarded the commission to build a bridge over the Awash and the water system for the royal palace in Addis Ababa. He also facilitated negotiations between Menelik and a French arms dealer named Arthur Rimbaud. The engineer was president of the Imperial Railway of Ethiopia that would soon link the capital with Djibouti. But business had not brought him to Lalibela, he confided as we sipped a syrupy hydromel. He had come to this holy city to visit its eleven Christian churches.

"What churches?" I said, surprised. "I haven't seen any steeples."

"All eleven churches are below ground," explained the engineer. "They were not built upward, but dug out and carved whole in the volcanic rock that lies beneath our feet. There is nothing like them anywhere in the world."

They were the work of King Lalibela himself, he added, who saw them in a vision when he was ill. Angels appeared to him in a dream and commanded him to build churches from a single stone.

"Faith not only moves mountains," said Alfred Ilg as we took leave of each other. "Sometimes it can dig deep into them as well. Don't fail to visit the churches. You will not be disappointed, I promise."

The next day I rose at dawn and set out along the path the engineer had pointed out to me, clambering up to the top of a hill west of the city. Thank God I had been looking straight ahead, for I suddenly found myself at the edge of a precipice, and I would have certainly fallen over it. At the bottom of this deep pit stood a church in the form of a Greek cross, whose roof was level with the earth. In a nearby trench, a stairway had been carved, and I gingerly descended its steep steps. Soon I found myself fifty feet below ground level, in front of a façade of red pumice hung with a shroud of greenish lichen. The church sat atop a massive pedestal; its severe lines were broken at regular intervals by apertures crowned by exquisite arabesques. The interior reflected the same variation of heaviness and lightness, from its roughly quarried pillars to the finely detailed frescoes that adorned its pediments. This startling place of pilgrimage was linked to its ten sisters by a labyrinth of trenches and tunnels whose walls were adorned with primitive frescoes, and honeycombed by countless grottoes in which troglodyte hermits had lodged through the ages. I felt as though I was wandering through an immense anthill, and almost expected to encounter a giant insect at every turn. Instead, I found myself face to face with the governess of the Ilg boy. Like the day before, she was wearing a close-fitting lace bodice and an Amazonian skirt that accentuated her hourglass figure. But what fascinated me most were her lips, which were separated by a deformity into two buccal appendages similar to the sharp-edged mandibles of a praying mantis.

"Are you looking for insects?" she asked in a voice whose inflections reminded me of a chirping cricket.

My heart leapt at her words, and I assailed her with questions. Had she seen the locusts? Were they far from here? Were there many left?

"The insects I have to show you are far rarer than the ones you are pursuing," she answered. "They are nesting in the last church, the Golgotha-Mikael. Allow me to take you there."

44

She did not have to ask twice. As we moved forward, the air grew cooler and the passageway so narrow that we had to turn sideways to slip through. I believe I mentioned, Father, that I was quite plump back then, and I was nearly trapped several times. Finally, we stopped in front of an opening so low I could not believe it was a door. To pass through it, I had to assume the prone position. The church's interior, totally devoid of all ornamentation, was feebly lit by the two candles the governess had brought along.

"Luckily there is no one here to see us," she whispered. "Foreigners are forbidden to enter Golgotha-Mikael."

We descended into a lateral crypt where three rectangular stone altars stood atop a podium. They looked oddly like three trunks abandoned on a railway station platform.

"This crypt carries the name of Selassie, which means 'power of the Trinity,' " explained the governess. "The most solemn ceremonies of the Ethiopian Church are celebrated here."

I took a candle from her and examined the altars.

"Where are the insects?" I asked.

"Farther along, in the mortuary chamber."

That chamber was situated in a niche that held two tombs, that of King Lalibela and, purportedly, of Adam himself. On a bas-relief, the latter was depicted without a navel, as tradition has it, since he was not born of a woman's womb and could not bear the original scar. Behind the tombs, a wide crevasse split the rock. According to the governess, it had opened during the recent earthquake.

"The earthquake was so violent that the bells of all eleven churches began to ring spontaneously," she added, then motioned me to move through.

I got down on all fours and tried to slip through the opening, but only my head and shoulders would fit. My protruding abdomen kept the rest of my body from following. In that uncomfortable position, I discovered that the crevasse opened onto a limestone grotto where dripping water had sculpted stalactites in the form of curtains, chandeliers, icicles and numerous other concretions. The ground was covered with a white substance I took to be limestone as well, until I saw it was a single seething mass. Had I been able to move, Father, I would have jumped for joy. Imagine, if you will: I found myself gazing at a colony of cave-dwelling locusts. Like all permanent inhabitants of the subterranean depths, they had lost their superfluous organs, and now had neither wings nor eyes. From lack of sunlight, their carapace had lost all pigmentation except for the pale blood that was visible. For how many millennia had these living fossils been trapped in this hermetic grotto, removed from the world, evolving in a closed system, creating their own laws, feeding on one another, degenerating through consanguine unions? They were like the Nephilim, those monstrous aborted fetuses born of the copulation of Guardian Angels with the Daughters of Man, which God banished to the darkest realms of Tartar until Judgment Day. I could have spent hours observing them, but the sulfurous atmosphere of the cave was intolerable for all but these curious creatures, and I was beginning to suffocate. I swept my open hand across the floor, hoping to capture several specimens. Sensing danger, the locusts retreated in waves beyond my reach, letting out strident cries. The governess promptly pulled me by my feet.

"What are you doing? You'll wake up the entire monastery!"

We stepped out of the church just in time to escape a group of threatening priests. I escorted the governess back to the inn and returned to my camp with a single idea in mind: to return to Golgotha-Mikael after night had fallen. I busied myself preparing everything I needed to capture the cave-dwelling locusts: nets, entomological pins and asphyxiation jars containing potassium cyanide covered with plaster of Paris. After supper I drank several cups of that excellent coffee from the high plateau, better to stay awake, and set off for the churches at the stroke of midnight. I met not a soul along the way. But as I drew closer to Golgotha-Mikael, I began to hear voices or, rather, a loud, high-pitched throbbing with an even rhythm that seemed to come from behind the church door. No sooner had I raised the latch than an onrushing, humming white swarm knocked me off my feet. The locusts were escaping! Pinned to the ground, I felt millions of tiny legs scrambling over my body, and could do nothing to stop them. Worse, the shock of their surge had put out my lantern. Once I could get to my feet, I blindly waved my net in hopes of capturing as many as possible. But the insects, with their extraordinary sensory perception, easily eluded me. With the first light of dawn, I discovered my net was empty. The swarm itself was already far away. And though I searched the grotto thoroughly, I didn't find even a single crushed locust.

I spent the rest of the day in my tent. My emotions ranged from fury to self-pity. I had come all the way to Ethiopia, and now I found myself like the grasshopper of the fable, without a sole morsel of fly or grub to my name. I would be the laughing-stock of my colleagues upon my return, and would certainly be dismissed from the experimental farm. As I was wondering how I could keep my membership in the Linnean Society, the governess stepped into my tent. I told her of my misfortune, but she did not seem to grasp the extent of my disarray.

"Forget those insects," she said with her praying-mantis smile. "I have something much better for you."

She unbuttoned her blouse and, before I could restrain her, she uncovered her navel. Be assured, Father, that I would have immediately averted my eyes had I not been struck by the unusual aspect of her abdominal scar. It appeared as a curious protrusion whose virgate shape, ringed form and worm-like contractions were quite familiar to me.

"I have a larva in my cavern," she said. "Would you like to see it?"

Taking up a magnifying glass, I drew closer. Indeed, in the governess's navel, a larva nestled. But a larva such as I had never seen. It resembled a hybrid embryo, issued from the obscene coupling of human and cricket. The membranes that covered its almond-shaped eyes were equipped with eyelashes, and two cartilaginous pinnae adorned each side of its head. The blood pumping through its mandibles gave them the appearance of fleshy lips. At the extremity of each leg wiggled five tiny, perfectly formed fingers. The Romans called larvae the malignant spirits that terrorized the living. They also believed that the larva is the mask of the perfect insect. What horrifying creature hid behind this mask? Certainly, it was not one known to science. At all costs, I had to get my hands on it and study it. I would present it to the Linnean Society, and my name would be inscribed in the great book of entomological taxonomy! Was not the discovery of a new species of insect, of an entirely new order, worth more than all the cave-dwelling locusts on earth? The governess seemed very attached to her larva, and it was all I could do to convince her to entrust it to me. Supplication and cajoling finally persuaded her to extract it from her umbilicus.

"This larva can live only on the human body," she said, placing it in my hand. "If you want to witness its metamorphosis, you must incubate it."

I spread my shirttails to receive the creature. After a second's hesitation, it scurried straight to my navel and burrowed in with a sucking sound. I felt a strange storm of sensations, as if my nerves were laid bare. Had someone spoken a hurtful word to me just then, I believe I would have burst into tears. And I did cry when the governess bid me farewell, for the Ilgs were returning to Addis-Ababa the following day. At suppertime I fed the larva with acacia pollen, then rocked it to sleep with a lullaby, dreaming of the prestigious name I would give it.

≈

Several days after leaving Lalibela, I noticed that I was eating with greater appetite than usual. At a single sitting, I could toss back an entire pot of lentils and a stack of *injera*, the large unleavened sheets of bread the Ethiopians also use as utensils. But that was not enough to satisfy me; an hour later, I felt hunger pangs again. My voracity did not come as a total surprise, for I had always been a hearty eater. However, I began losing rather than gaining weight. On several occasions during the return trip to Djibouti, I had to tighten my belt a notch or two to keep my trousers from slipping. Happily, the larva I bore was growing by leaps and bounds. It now formed a slight protuberance on the surface of my abdomen.

The Atlantic crossing was far more unpleasant. In the clutches of hunger that never abated, I swallowed down everything the seasick passengers left on their plates, at the risk of being judged the most insatiable of gluttons. Yet I was still famished, and my clothing hung upon my limbs. The only food that seemed to calm my ravenous appetite was fish. Which is why I took up fishing once I returned. Collecting bait was child's play, for the larva began to secrete a sweet, honey-like substance that attracted all insects: flies, mosquitoes, bumblebees, wasps, beetles and dragonflies. They whirred about me unceasingly, circling my umbilical region like staggering drunkards, but never attacking me. I had become like King Lalibela. Was I fated to turn into He Whom the Insects Respect, and reign over the distinguished subjects of my profession? My anxiety increased as I waited for the larva's metamorphosis.

Several weeks passed and, despite my frequent excesses at table, I was no more than skin and bones. Fearing I had contracted an intestinal parasite, I stuffed myself with vermifuges. I tried absinthe, pumpkin seeds, extract of fern, cabbage gum, wormseed, tansy, all with no result. Faced with a wall of evidence, I could draw only one conclusion: the Ilg's governess had deceived me. The creature she passed on to me was not even an insect, since it never reached the nymphal stage. It was the worst kind of parasite siphoning off my vital energy. Perhaps it was a liver fluke waiting for the right moment to burrow into the ducts of my gallbladder or, worse yet, a screwworm that would climb my spinal cord to my skull cavity and devour my brain. I had to abort this disastrous experiment with no further delay.

I thought a few contractions would be enough to expel the parasite from my navel. A grievous error. The creature had developed a pair of buccal pincers with which it had anchored itself to my flesh, resisting even the pressure of forceps. I then tried to dislodge it by flooding my umbilical cavity with a saline solution. It twisted briefly, but did not release its hold. Desperate times call for desperate measures, I decided. I soaked a cotton swab in turpentine and applied it to the opening for fifteen minutes. I observed no reaction, so I repeated the treatment, first with mineral oil, then with ether, chloroform, ethyl alcohol and calomel. As a last resort, I opened a small bottle of sulfuric acid. I felt a tickling sensation at the bottom of my umbilicus, but the parasite quickly fell asleep. At wit's end, I was all but resigned to letting it devour me. But this morning, the solution came to me unexpectedly. I was fishing in the shade of a willow. Sitting on my folding stool, I watched the river rippled by the breeze. Suddenly it occurred to me that a parasite is not much different from a fish. To catch it, all you need is the proper bait. Since mine seemed quite fond of everything I ingested, I attached a small morsel of perch to the end of my line and held it above my navel. The parasite immediately lifted its head from its hole and took the hook. So it would suspect nothing as it swallowed the bait, I let out the line, then pitilessly drove the hook home. I had no time to savor my victory. A violent whirlpool whipped the surface of the river, and a huge muskellunge split the water. With one bite, it swallowed the parasite and dove into the depths again. The line tensed and the pole nearly bent double as I held on for dear life. My enemy fought so ferociously that it was all I could do to control the reel. Finally, after a lengthy battle, I managed to bring it to shore. I searched its mouth to remove the hook, but the fish had swallowed it whole. How the devil was I to bring a monster of that size home? It did not fit in my landing net, or in my creel. I had no choice but to gut and fillet it on the spot. I laid the muskellunge on the grass, took out my knife and thrust it into the fish's white belly. Its viscera spilled out and, in the midst, I spotted my parasite. It was still very much alive, wallowing between the glossy lobes of the liver, sucking up the dark coagulating blood. It shuddered and, from its genital orifice, released a dozen eggs before curling up once more.

Like the snail, the leech and the earthworm, this creature was hermaphrodite. Either that, or it was able to reproduce without a male, through parthenogenesis ... Horrified, I watched as the eggs hatched. The young not only looked more human than their mother, but had inherited my features!

Please take no offense, Father, for I would like to pause briefly for some sustenance. You can't imagine how satisfying it is to once again eat my fill, free of that parasite that deprived me of all nutrition. Can I offer you a slice of bread, or perhaps a bit of this excellent muskellunge? See how delicate the flesh is, almost translucent ... All the same, I don't have much appetite for fish. I have even decided to give up fishing for a time. I won't be needing my bait or my countless lures. If you wish, I will give them to you most happily. I'm even willing to pass on the parasite that no muskellunge can resist, for you will know how to use it best. So great is my trust in you that I brought it with me, along with its offspring. I carried them in this hamper, but since I feared they would devour my meal, I put them in a safe place before entering the confessional. They are creatures that live in darkness, and a single ray of sunlight, even filtered through a stained-glass window, is enough to kill them. To avoid exposing them unduly to light, I placed them in the white-gold pyx stored in the tabernacle. You will find them lying flaccidly upon the hosts, the edges of which they will most certainly have begun to nibble, their white-ringed bodies reflected endlessly on the gilded sides of the bowl ... I know it is a sacrilege to place a parasite in a sanctified object used to transport the hosts for communion for the sick, but if we consider it more closely, is not the Eucharist a kind of bait hiding the hook of salvation by which Christ attracts the lost small fry back to the divine landing net? You will notice that upon the lid of your pyx is engraved the word "*ichthys*," which is the monogram signifying "Jesus Christ, Son of God, Savior" in Greek, which also means "fish" in that language. I trust you will be so indulgent as to grant me absolution for this trivial profanation.

INCENSUM NEFARIUM

LOWER YOUR EYES, FATHER. Lower. Lower still. In the shadows, can you make out my body stretched prone, face to the ground? I would like to claim that my prostration is a sign of humility and deepest repentance. In truth, I am driven to it by a chronic affliction. I suffer from such debilitating vertigo that I cannot even kneel without swaying back and forth on my patellae. As I am tall, standing erect is a constant torment. To come here, I had to walk bent double, more hunched than an old man. The women I encountered found me courtly in the extreme. At home, I do not burden myself with such niceties: I sleep under my bed and, to move about, I slither laterally like a snake. You have no idea how hard this is on my clothing. I'm forced to wear a leather breastplate and kneepads! I would never have the strength, as you have, to ascend to the pulpit each time a homily must be delivered. Hanging between heaven and earth, gazing down upon the crowded pews, I would be terrified of plummeting down upon the hundreds of attentive faces turned toward me. In any case, I rarely attend Mass any more, though I am a pious person and never miss the occasion to celebrate the Ascension of Our Savior, even if the smell of incense indisposes me. It lifts my soul toward the heavens, but then I feel cast down from on high when I descend once more into this vile world. So powerfully do I dread the moment when the priest swings the incensory as he circumambulates the altar that I shall never make the pilgrimage to Saint James of Compostela. There, they display an incensory that measures a full five feet tall and weighs nearly two hundred pounds, the Botafumeiro, which can fill the entire cathedral with smoke. It hangs suspended from the dome by a rope attached to a pulley. To make it swing back and forth, eight men pull on the rope, which creates a parametric oscillation that makes the incensory swing like a pendulum from one end of the transept to the other. The advantage is that the smell masks the incommodious odor of the pilgrims, but I would never survive such a stern test.

The incensory of your parish, though it does not have the dimensions of the Botafumeiro, is no less precious. It is made of solid silver, if I am not mistaken, and previously belonged to the legendary collection of the Jesuits, which was dispersed in 1800 after the Order was suppressed by Pope Clement xiv. The protection of such a piece must be a constant source of concern for you, which is why I have come to warn you: your treasure is in grave danger! A short time ago, a woman took advantage of a time when the church was empty to slip into the choir. She was not a thief, but her intentions were just as malevolent. Not suspecting that I was following her, she approached the credenza in her slightly trotting gait and deposited a handful of red pearls in the incense carrier, then slipped out the side door. If by inadvertence you had placed these highly resinous pearls on the burning coals of the incensory, they would have thrown off sparks and emitted an irradiating heat that would have quickly exceeded the melting point of silver. Even if you lowered the lid or doused it with holy water, you would not have been able to smother the combustion. That would have been the end of your fine Jesuit incensory! Deformed! Ruined! No choice but to melt it down.

Fear not, Father; I have recovered the pearls of incense. Allow me to hand them to you through the screen. Examine them at your leisure, but resist the temptation to smell them. The odor of musk that comes from them is so divine it is diabolical; it is the odor of the warm, carnal folds of sin itself. These tiny reddish beads have nothing in common with pontifical incense, a mixture of myrrh, gum benzoin and storax that has the appearance of gunpowder. Nor is it the famed frankincense that King Gaspar brought as a gift to the Infant Jesus. Olibanum in its pure state is derived from a shrub that grows in the southern Arabian peninsula, *Boswellia sacra*, whose bark is tapped in the fall to collect the drops of resin that it exudes and which, in drying, turn opaque and odoriferous. Frankincense is known as "male incense," for only the male boswellia shrub yields it. What you are now holding in your hand is female incense. It is so rare that it cannot be found either on this continent or in the Old World.

I was initiated into the mysteries of female incense while traveling in Yemen. I had gone there in search of the vertical cities of the desert, for I hoped to find the solution to the problem of tall structures. I don't believe I mentioned that architecture is my passion. For as far back as I can remember, the chapter in Genesis on the Tower of Babel has fascinated me. I dreamed of building houses that would reach the clouds, and could not understand why Montreal's proudest structure, the New York Life Insurance Company on the place d'Armes, boasted of a mere ten storeys. My godfather, a construction contractor, explained to me that masonry walls become progressively unstable the higher they rise. Past a certain limit, they will collapse like a house of cards if they are not supported by abutments and flying buttresses. Masons in the Middle Ages tried to remedy this weakness by sacrificing human beings. They believed that if a victim were buried alive in the foundations of a building, it would never fall. Evidence of this barbarous rite is not difficult to uncover: beneath the stones of two round towers in Ireland, human skeletons have been found, and archeological excavations have proven that, as recently as the fifteenth century, a child was mixed into the mortar of a church in Britain. Today, thank God, we do no more than deposit, in a hollow stone, a few coins and a newspaper to assuage these superstitions. My godfather, wanting to encourage my vocation, apprenticed me to an architectural firm once I had finished college. When the time came to prepare my entrance examinations for the Royal Institute, he was generous enough to pay for courses with Stewart Capper, an eminent professor trained in Edinburgh and at the École des Beaux-Arts in Paris. Capper was a man of great refinement, always exquisitely – not to say effeminately – dressed. He spoke seven or eight languages, including Arabic, and often pontificated in Latin or Ancient Greek. His studio, situated on the uppermost floor of the McGill University engineering faculty, was filled with scale models of the wonders of the classical era: the Theater of Marcellus, the Temple of Vesta at Tivoli, the Erechtheion Portal … By his own admission, he had dreamed of becoming an archeologist. He maintained a frequent correspondence with many members of that profession, and had begun a friendship with the great traveler Theodore Bent, the author of works on the subterranean churches of Ethiopia and the ruins of Mashonaland. Always quite paternal with his protégés, Capper congratulated me warmly when, at year's end, I reported that I had successfully passed my examinations. He invited me into his office and asked what I intended to do next. I told him of my intention to complete my studies in Chicago, where they had begun to use steel structures that made it possible to superpose as many as eighteen floors.

"Eighteen is a substantial number," Capper said, gazing at me from above his lorgnette. "But there is a place where buildings are taller still."

Picking up a venerable volume that lay before him, he opened it to the page indicated by a bookmark and turned it toward me. The text was in German. Capper explained that it was the account of a journey to Arabia by the explorer Carsten Niebuhr around 1760, during which he lost all those who accompanied him. He translated a passage in which the explorer related having seen, in the realm of Sheba, buildings made of sand whose seven or eight rooms each occupied a different floor. Niebuhr had also heard that in the south of the peninsula, in the valley of Hadramaut, towered an entire city made of square towers whose height rivaled the surrounding mountains. I could not hide an incredulous frown.

"If such a city existed," I replied to the professor, "we would surely have heard of it."

Capper shook his head as he settled into his armchair. Several moments passed before he answered, time enough to adjust the red fez whose silk tassel had fallen over his forehead.

"Neither Alexander the Great nor the Emperor Augustus was able to conquer this fertile region that ancient geographers called Happy Arabia, *Arabia Felix*, to contrast it with the Arabia of the desert and the Arabia of stones. The tribes that occupy Hadramaut today have lost nothing of their ferocity, particularly toward the outside world. They are Moslem and inflict the penalty of death upon any infidel whose impure presence would sully the sacred soil trodden by the Prophet Mohammed. Not even Niebuhr dared set foot there. My friend

Theodore Bent, on the other hand, found a way to enter that land."

The professor read me a letter he had just received from the great traveler who described having made, in Hyderabad, the acquaintance of Sultan Nawasjung al-Kaiti. The sultan was a man of immeasurable wealth, and reigned over the entire valley of Hadramaut, but did not reside there, preferring life with the British Army of the Indies, whose Arab regiment he commanded. He left the care of his lands to his son and his nephew. He had promised the archeologist his protection if he wished to explore them. Needless to say, Bent accepted the invitation and was preparing to travel to Yemen. He was looking for an excellent draughtsman who could make a pictorial record of the ruins his excavations would reveal, and had proposed that Capper join him. The latter's obligations made it impossible, unfortunately, for him to accept, but he was willing to recommend me to his friend. How could I let such an opportunity pass me by? Instead of taking the train to Chicago, I took passage on a steamship.

~

I disembarked at the port of al-Mukalla on November 4. Theodore Bent, who had been informed of my arrival by the Aden telegraph, awaited me on the quay, at a safe distance from the fishmongers and the pelicans. He was a man of sturdy build, his face hidden by a flowing beard and an overlong toupee. Despite the heat, he was clad in a woolen suit of houndstooth pattern, and wore a polka-dot tie knotted tightly around his neck. He introduced me to his wife Mabel, a green-eyed Irishwoman, who accompanied him on all his expeditions. Leaving his dutiful Greek servant Matthaios the task of fetching my bags, Theodore Bent led me through the city, pointing out the sultan's palace, a mosque whose minaret was speckled with pigeon droppings and the market stalls where Bombay Parsis sold silver-plated hookahs. The Bents had taken up residence in a bungalow hidden behind a row of tamarisks. In their pink-hued shade, I made the acquaintance of the other members of the expedition: William Lunt, the London botanist affiliated with Kew Gardens; Mahmoud Bayoumi, the Egyptian naturalist recommended by Cairo University; and Imam Sherif, a topographer and scion of a noble Arab family who spoke eight languages, including an English superior to mine. Their welcome was polite but no more and, had it not been for Bent's kindness, I would have had an unpleasant time of it. Their coldness toward me was almost cordial compared to what prevailed between them. They sized each other up, kept close watch over one another and uttered sarcastic asides. At first I attributed the hostility to professional rivalry, but soon grasped the true reason when the three leapt to their feet at the sound of an approaching pair of high heels.

I expected to see a dark-eyed, full-hipped *houri* make her appearance. Instead, a pale-skinned, fine-featured young woman made her entrance onto the veranda. Not at all disagreeable to look at, please understand me, but disfigured by a deep gash in her upper lip – a congenital defect resulting from a malformation of the palate, the professor whispered to me. She was wearing a turban in the oriental style that covered not only her hair, but her ears as well – a display of coquetry that considerably diminished her ability to hear. To engage her in conversation, one had to come very close to her, which gave her suitors an excuse to cluster around her like flies to honey. Mrs. Bent had met her in Muscat at a dinner party at the governor's. What was she doing without a chaperone in this garrison town? She had opened a photography studio, and took pictures of military men! A few days later, the two women had met again by the cisterns, the only place where a touch of coolness could be found when the sun beat down on the volcanic rocks. Since then, they had been inseparable. Mrs. Bent invited her new friend to join the expedition as photographer, and the young woman accepted. I kept my doubts about the wisdom of such a decision to myself, thinking that the three roosters were more than likely to cross beaks again.

Matthaios served us tea in gilt-rimmed glasses, with dates and other honeyed delicacies too sweet for my taste, but that pleased the ladies. Once they finished their nibbling, the professor announced that, after lengthy negotiations, the Sultan of Muscat had granted us safe conduct, as well as lending us twenty-two camels.

"Prepare yourselves, for we are leaving for Hadramaut the day after tomorrow."

Though peace had reputedly returned to the region since the crucifixion of several rebel chiefs, the sultan placed our security in the hands of the head of the Khaliki Bedouins, a superb brigand who answered to the name of Mokaik. As Bedouins were not allowed into the city, we joined him outside the walls, at dawn. Showing no consideration for the ladies, he wore only a loincloth and a belt from which hung a dagger, a powder horn, a flint and various pincers used to remove hair. His curly locks were secured at the back of his head with a leather thong, and his beardless face was lined with streaks of indigo. Once his men had finished loading the bundles of dried fish on which the camels would feed, he gave the signal for departure, and we set off for the valley of Hadramaut. It did not take me long to understand why the name meant "death on foot." The route was the same as the Bedouins had used for centuries for the incense trade. Crossing high plateaus, it skirted gorges surmounted by ramparts of basalt, blacker than coal. Then it wound its way through desert not of sand, but of sharp-edged stone shards through which the camels picked their way in single file. For twenty days we marched beneath a scorching sun, dismounting only at dusk, when the ticks of our mounts began to devour us whole. Each of us retired to his tent, with nothing more to drink than a bowl of camel's milk, since we rarely had permission to dip our infidel flasks into the springs in the hamlets through which we passed. Had I hoped to broaden my acquaintance with my colleagues during the journey, I would have certainly been disappointed. One night, when thirst and the irritating tick bites made sleep impossible, I went for a walk through the bivouac, taking care not to stumble over the entanglement of tent poles. As I drew near the fire where Mokaik and his men were gathered, I was surprised to see Mrs. Bent's friend among them. I was about to move off when she trained her eyes on me and beckoned me to join her. I took a few steps in her direction and was overwhelmed by a perfume so heady and so overwhelming that you would have to be a Bedouin or suffering from a bad head cold to tolerate it. The smell did not come from the dried camel dung our caravan used as fuel, but from a small incense tree that had caught fire and was burning with a crackling sound. Its flame lit the face of the young woman who seemed overcome by torpor, no doubt induced by the smoke that the wind carried in her direction.

"Do you see how this boswellia burns without being consumed?" she said. "Perhaps the burning bush in which Moses believed he saw God was simply an incense tree?"

I know, Father, that I should have admonished her for uttering such disrespectful remarks. But I was seeing her for the first time without her turban, and my attention was completely captivated by her earlobes, for the glimmer of firelight cast their abnormal form in sharp relief. The circumvolutions of cartilage formed a perfect helix at the tip of each lobe, and the vortex with its spirals drew me into the mysterious orifice of her ear canal. I would have liked to place my eye against it, as against a keyhole; through a kind of subtle intuition, suddenly I was sure I would find the key to new architectures there. I was so shaken by this vision that I did not react when our photographer slipped away with Mokaik and disappeared into his tent.

I remember little of the final stages of the journey, probably because what occurred next erased any impressions I might have formed. I know we celebrated the New Year near the ruins of Meshed, an ancient Himyarite city half-buried in sand. Its stones bore numerous inscriptions in honor of the dead, of which I made copies while the professor carried out his excavations. A few days later, we wound our way down into the valley of Hadramaut. The damp wadi and the cool shade of the palms along its banks felt like Eden recovered after having endured the burning, arid plateaus. We saw many women at work in the fields. Wearing high, peaked hats and very short, indigo skirts that revealed their yellow-tinted legs, they were planting millet while the men lounged about, slouched in front of their houses, passing the time of day by chewing the leaves of a shrub called *khat*. If, as they claim, the leaves are a stimulant, I never witnessed that effect on those ne'er-do-wells. We came across small villages only, and I was beginning to despair of ever beholding the vertical cities. But my hopes were revived when, in mid-January, we reached the palace of Salah al-Kaiti: the princely residence was built into the flank of a cliff and stood five storeys high! The sultan, who was then the most powerful man in Hadramaut, had spent twelve years in India close to his uncle Nawasjung without, however, losing his taste for Arab manners and customs. He received us on a goat's-hair carpet, and served us Moka coffee sweetened with date-flower honey. When it came my turn to address him, I first praised the beauty of his palace. I then asked him if he could confirm the existence of the desert's vertical cities.

"You must mean Shibam," he answered, stroking his noble beard. "I was not aware that its reputation had reached your lands."

Raising himself from the divan on which he reclined, he got to his feet and led me onto the terrace that overlooked the surrounding countryside. He showed me a point upstream of the wadi that seemed no more than a lone tumulus in the midst of the valley. But through my field glasses, the contours of the tumulus took shape and my eyes made out a sight they would have considered to be a mirage: an entire city, immense, made of houses taller than towers, next to which the palm trees looked like miniature shrubs. Judging by the number of windows, those houses must have stood at least twenty storeys tall. Until then, I had not taken the proper measure of my desire to one day reach the vertical cities of the desert. I began to imagine the consequences such a discovery would have in my life. I pictured myself returning home, crowned with glory, becoming the master builder of the most imposing edifices ever known, my name inscribed in gold letters in the Great Book of architecture. I told the sultan of my intention to visit Shibam as soon as possible.

"I will accompany you tomorrow," he said. "For the people there are closed-minded, and hostile to outsiders. If you attempted to enter the city alone, they would slit your throat on sight."

The sultan had placed at our disposition a suite of private apartments on the uppermost floor of the palace, where the ladies withdrew for their afternoon nap. While my colleagues went off to explore the shores of the wadi, I set out on a stroll to the neighboring village. At the entrance to the bazaar, a toothless old man accosted me in an attempt to sell me all manner of stuff and baubles. I was about to send him away when I heard, in the midst of his blather, "*al-luban,*" the Arabic term for olibanum. I saw an opportunity to enter the confidence of the young woman with the spiral ears. Gesticulating, I sought to indicate my interest to the old man. His face lit up and, from a hammered copper case, he drew a handful of large beads of resin of immaculate whiteness – a sign, according to what I had heard, of the highest quality. Only incense harvested at the autumn solstice has that milky, slightly powdery aspect; spring incense is amber and far less pungent. I didn't even bother bargaining. I handed over all the coins in my possession to the merchant and took leave of him with the incense beads wrapped in my handkerchief. I did not wait for the afternoon nap to end; I tapped on our photographer's door, sure that she would admit me. I surprised her as she was getting out of bed, in her negligee, disheveled. Before she could show me the door, I quickly produced the contents of my handkerchief.

"This is male incense," she said after taking in its perfume, "and of exceptional quality."

"I am something of a connoisseur," I stated, and thrust my chest out ever so slightly. No exaggeration would stop me from putting my best foot forward.

"Really?" she answered, inviting me in. "What do you know of female incense?"

66

The truth is that I knew precious little, except that it is less prized than olibanum, is extracted from the juniper plant and presents itself in the form of small seeds. In certain ancient civilizations, it was reserved for anointing those who had died by their own hand.

The lady interrupted my explanation.

"I am speaking of true female incense."

She beckoned me to sit on the carpet next to her. I was in the perfect position to examine her ears, and wondered what fallacious pretext I might use to move even closer. Meanwhile, on a tray, she was setting out a marble thurible and a goblet of reddish pearls that she let slip between her fingers.

"This incense is a bit dry," she said disdainfully. "The fresher variety would be more suitable for the occasion."

Taking the brooch that served to fasten her blouse, she opened the fastener and, holding the jewel's pin between her thumb and index finger, stabbed it into her ear. I let out a cry of horror, but my companion showed not the slightest emotion. Quite the contrary: she continued thrusting the pin deeper into her ear canal, manipulating it with such skill that she soon pulled out, thanks to that most unusual instrument, a ball of cerumen the size of a pearl.

In humans, there are two varieties of cerumen, as different as two distinct humors. In some individuals the cerumen is moist and drains naturally from the ear without having to remove it. But in others, it is dry and forms grayish flakes that, when they accumulate, obstruct the canal and diminish the ability to hear. Our photographer's variety was of a completely different nature. Perfectly spherical, it had the resinous appearance of colophony and the color of burning coals.

"This incense must be burned in marble," she said, "for it can reach the temperature of lava and would melt any metallic recipient."

By simply rubbing it, she set the pearl alight, and it began sending out languid, opaque, almost viscous smoke that hugged the floor like autumn fog instead of rising into the air. Its dark arabesques slipped into my nasal passages with a telluric vibration that shook the very depths of my ears. My sense of balance failed, and I was overcome by exquisite vertigo that, in my incautiousness, I sought only to prolong. Mind reeling, I leaned over the young woman's ear canal, and my gaze sank deep into it as into a burrow. A succession of endless galleries threw themselves open as I advanced, crossing vestibules cluttered with roots and chambers bathed in a reddish light, stepping over bottomless pits, emerging into dungeons and attics hung with drying herbs. I journeyed down a tunnel, ever deeper, under the earth's crust, where rivers of lava flow and ponds of magma bubble. Had I reached the subbasement of Hell? I had no concern for anything but the complexities of this subterranean architecture that inspired me with a hundred projects and a thousand plans. I saw myself as the master builder of a buried city where men would crawl among moles, worms and ants. And what more appropriate tribute could there be to my honor than this perfumed homage from so precious a source? Just then, Mrs. Bent's lady friend shook me from my torpor and handed me the marble cupel.

"Take as many as you wish," she said as I filled my pockets with cerumen. "But be careful. Never burn more than one pearl at a time."

I left her room with my head spinning, using the walls to steady myself. Never, until then, had I suffered from vertigo. Quite the opposite: I had always prided myself on being light of foot. But now the earth seemed to slip away beneath my feet, and the very thought of standing at the top of a five-storey palace only increased my panic. A single desire took hold of me: I wanted to sink to the carpet and never get up. Come sunset, I was still unsteady and, in hopes of regaining some stability, I committed the error of burning a pearl of incense. My sleep that night was fitful, interrupted by frequent periods of wakefulness during which I sought, in the blind darkness, the entrance to a burrow of some kind. In the morning, I emerged from my room stunned, confused and in ill humor. But I did my best to put on a good countenance for the sultan who had marshaled a substantial force for our expedition to Shibam. The journey was unpleasant; the camel assigned to me stood so tall I was in constant fear of falling off. At last I spied the vertical city that no Western eye had ever beheld. Imagine a citadel of five hundred square, crenellated towers, more than a hundred feet high, separated from one another by passages so narrow that not a ray of sunlight could penetrate, offering the five thousand inhabitants a constant cool atmosphere. The city gates, usually shut because Shibam was at war with some neighboring tribe, had been thrown open that morning to receive the sultan and his retinue. They opened onto a small, congested square; there, we had to make our way through tubs of indigo and heaps of unfired bricks. The bricks, made of alfalfa and silt, provided Shibam with its main construction material. They were laid atop a foundation of cut stone, with a fine mud coating as mortar, and protected from the elements by a thick layer of whitewash.

The towers themselves were wonders of primitive construction, perhaps even as impressive in their own way as the mosque at Timbuktu or the great mud-brick citadel of Bam. But in no way could they rival the skyscrapers of Chicago that stood twice as high. In fact, they numbered ten floors and not twenty, as I had believed, since each floor had two rows of windows, one at floor level and a second row of clerestory windows near the ceiling for light. Still, I was eager to visit the towers, so the sultan led me to one of the town's notables with whom he had dealings, and who threw open the doors of his residence to me. The ground floor was reserved for the livestock, and the first and second were used as storerooms. The men's quarters occupied the next three floors. The women, who never went into the street, were cloistered on high, but could visit their neighbors via an ingenious system of covered catwalks. I climbed to the roof that boasted of a terrace whose privacy was guarded by a latticework of tamarind wood screens. Curious to see how high I really was, I made the mistake of peeking through an opening. The tower at whose summit I was perched suddenly began to sway on its foundations, threatening to fall and knock over its neighbors like so many dominoes. Worse still, the street below came surging up toward me. With a cry of fright, I leapt back and rushed to the stairway, but it was folding and unfolding like an accordion as if it wanted to dash my skull on the bottom step. I had to go down backward, with my eyes closed. Leaving the sultan to converse with our host, I sought refuge on the ground floor, among the goats. Discouraged, overwhelmed, a wreck surrounded by droppings, I had nothing more to cling to outside of one pearl of female incense I had slipped into my pocket. I burned it, and immediately felt better. As did the goats, apparently, since they ceased their bleating and lay down beside me. That's when I had an illumination: all of man's constructions, since the beginning of time, had been monumental errors. Had we not learned our lesson from the Tower of Babel? It was insanity to build buildings that constantly struggled against gravity. Instead, we should follow the example of small mammals and burrow out subterranean cities, oriented not toward the sun, but toward the earth's igneous core. Below ground we would be protected against heat and frost. We would not have to fight erosion caused by wind and rain. The world would once again be as it was before man's fall.

Since my return from Yemen, I have been trying to apply this new architectural principle, thanks to my godfather's generous bequest. I have begun modestly, with a burrow that stretches beneath my garden. Yesterday I completed the main galleries and the larder. A few more rooms and I will be able to move in. On that day, I will level my house, needless to say.

When at last I am living below ground, I will no longer be plagued by vertigo. I will not need these pearls of incense. Take them, Father, they will be more useful to you than me. I have often heard you deliver the homily. I know how much you enjoy standing high in the pulpit, better to display your oratorical talents. You prolong your sermons by adding figures of speech, you take delight in threatening the faithful whose faces you know well, since you have studied them from the corner of your eye through the confessional screen. Bless this incense. May it be for you a perfume of consolation and grace. May its smoke dispel all evil thoughts from your soul and your body. Burn a pearl now, Father. Never again will you yield to the temptations of the pulpit.

V

OCULUS MALIGNUS

WHERE ARE YOU, FATHER? In the confessional your voice resounds and its echo comes from all directions at once. I feel for the screen like a poor pin-the-tail-on-the-donkey player, for I am not blind from birth. My infirmity is still too new to have given way to habit, and my memory of the world is nothing more than the final images that were printed on my retina before this degenerative condition turned my corneas opaque. One of these images I hope never to forget are the turtles coming ashore to lay their eggs on the beaches of the Daymaniyat Islands.

I had the privilege of witnessing this extraordinary event, having been dispatched to the Sultanate of Oman by my employer, Mr. Thomas Parker of Parker and Son, official purveyor to His Excellency Lord Aberdeen, our Right Honorable Governor General. You are aware of that elegant establishment in Dominion Square that sells tortoiseshell eyeglasses, since you yourself are among its most loyal clients. I don't need to point out to you that spectacles and monocles, lorgnettes and pince-nez, by virtue of their frequent use, are subject to breakage of all kinds. Which is why, in the rear of his establishment, Mr. Parker opened a repair shop operated by a venerable Austrian craftsman, Herr Linke, who long worked in the Faubourg Saint-Antoine, with the highly renowned Parisian furniture maker Gabriel Viardot. With him, Linke mastered the art of Buhl work, which consists of inlaying tortoiseshell on a copper base, before going on to specialize in plaquette marquetry. He had the honor of restoring a mantilla comb that had belonged to an infanta of Spain, as well as one of the treasures of the Pau Castle, the turtle shell that had served as a cradle for the future King Henri IV of France. At Parker's, where I worked as a clerk, Herr Linke often called upon me for small jobs. Because of the interest I demonstrated, he undertook to teach me how to plate tortoiseshell.

Only sea turtles yield the extremely fine shell used in the manufacture of eyeglasses: among them, the hawksbill turtle is the most sought-after because of its honey-colored scutes, which make them the rarest and most prized. Though Parker had no difficulty procuring pink- or cherry-colored tortoiseshell, obtaining blond shell was an entirely different matter. The fine furniture makers and marquetry artists of Europe had first call for the lightest-colored pieces, and exporters would send us only the leavings – brownish plates from hawksbill feet, of no value whatsoever. The monocles worn by our client Lord Aberdeen were all fashioned from blond shell. In an effort not to lose his commission, Mr. Parker decided to send me to Oman, for it is there that the hawksbill come to reproduce once a year, between April and September. At the end of the lunar cycle, when the tide is at its lowest, the females come upon the beaches by the tens of thousands and, with powerful scoops of their feet, dig holes in the sand where, over several hours, they deposit some four dozen eggs before returning to sea. The hunters lie in wait for them on the beach with their harpoons and nets. The hawksbill, which in water fear no predator, rarely escape the hecatomb.

Muscat, which I had never heard of before my commission there, is apparently the most ancient of all cities of the Middle

East. It is situated on what was once called the Pirate Coast, at the head of a bay almost entirely enclosed by a precipitous rocky promontory crowned by the al-Jalali Fortress. In this impregnable citadel, accessible only by a steep staircase carved from the rock itself, lived the British consul, the supreme authority after Sultan Faisal bin Turki, the first sovereign of Oman not to have usurped the throne. Wishing to assure myself the consul's protection, I presented myself once I'd disembarked, carrying a letter of introduction signed by Lord Aberdeen himself. I was handsomely received in an apartment cooled by twelve broad punkahs suspended from the ceiling, each operated by a boy who stirred the air above our heads with his steady movement. The consul was a diminutive, worried man who moved about with cold compresses on his forehead, for he feared the devastating effect of the heat on his insular organism. His concerns were not unfounded, he assured me. In the register of the consulate, one could read that the Muscat climate had driven one of his predecessors mad, and another had been "murdered by sunstroke."

"Leave this place as soon as you are able," he advised me. "Otherwise you may find it impossible to do so."

When I told him I could not depart before first acquiring a sufficient quantity of tortoiseshell, he warned me against the Muscat traders, all of whom were, according to him, scheming rascals as unscrupulous in business as they were avid profiteers. He recommended the services of a certain Salem bin-Nizar al-Balouchi, a turtle fisherman recognized for his honesty and affability toward foreigners – apparently a rare quality among the harbor rabble – and told me where I could find his vessel.

When I left the al-Jalili Fortress, I simply followed the porters loaded with rods of antimony and senna leaves, and so reached the wharves. I made my way between green doves and drying shark fins waiting to be shipped to China until I caught sight of Salem al-Balouchi on the deck of his dhow, industriously caulking the scuppers with fish oil. He reeked from twenty feet away, but he was the only fisherman who did not carry on his belt one of those long, curved scimitars that could slice open your throat with one swipe – which immediately inspired my confidence. Not only did he appear quite amicably disposed toward me, but insisted I be his guest for the length of my stay. I did not dare refuse his hospitality, and took up quarters in the room he offered me, a salon of modest dimensions but irreproachably clean, furnished with a narrow daybed, several cushions and a mirror in a carved wooden frame. We set out on our expedition the following afternoon, first having ingurgitated a copious repast of camel stew and goat's belly spiced with cardamom. It would have been simpler to remain in the vicinity of Muscat, but Salem insisted on taking me to the Daymaniyat Islands, where the greatest schools of hawksbill turtles come ashore to lay their eggs. Dusk was falling as we caught sight of the coast. From our dhow, the shore looked inhospitable, hardly propitious as a nesting ground, for it was strewn with large boulders where a broad beach should have been. But my apprehension quickly turned to wonderment when I grasped that the beach was, in fact, black with turtles. If it had not been for the surrounding reefs, we could have put ashore and simply bent over to capture them barehanded.

"Patience," said Salem as he dropped anchor. "At dawn they will return to the water and come to us."

The new day had hardly broken, and already we had captured a dozen turtles each weighing more than 150 pounds – more than the boat could hold. Lying on their backs, the miserable creatures struggled mightily to turn themselves over, snapping at the air with beaks as curved as a hawk's, and trying to bite anything that came within range. With one swift stroke of his cutlass, Salem sliced open their cuirasses as though they were oysters, separating the ventral plastron from the shell covered with eighteen medallions, each superposed atop the other like the stones of a slate roof. The butchered carcasses were immediately thrown back to sea, for the hawksbill feed on sponges and venomous Portuguese man-of-war that make their flesh too toxic even for shark bait. As I helped stack the carapaces on the floor of the dhow, I admired their glistening, multicolored patterns that had nothing in common with the dull brownish leaves that until then had come into my possession. Still, I maintained my composure, knowing that the plaques were no thicker than a finger and that, once detached from their bony base, might weigh no more than two pounds. Considering how great Mr. Parker's order was, I still had a full turtle-hunting season before me.

~

Near the end of February, I was ready to return home with all the shell I needed. I went to the offices of the Orient Lines and booked passage on the ss *Ophir*, which was currently docked in Muscat for repairs and would be sailing in eight days for England, via Aden and the Suez Canal. I then paid a call on the consul to bid farewell. Still wearing a cold compress on his head, that day he was receiving a group of missionaries who had arrived from Damascus on the same ship upon which I would soon be embarking – eight men and three women, all clad in the same light-colored coats with epaulets and woven leather buttons. They were going to visit the citadel, and I was graciously invited to join them. Built in 1552 during the Portuguese occupation, the citadel had been enlarged by several subsequent sultans, who had transformed it in such a way as to confuse any enemy who succeeded in entering. The consul suggested we follow our guide (one of the boys who operated the punkahs), failing which our bleached bones would be discovered years later. Out of courtesy, I allowed the missionaries to precede me, and brought up the rear.

We first made our way up a series of narrow stairways, then passed through an armory, followed a zigzagging corridor, and then entered a succession of blind redoubts that led to yet more stairways and passages veering now to the left, now to the right, as if following the directions of a panicky weather vane. The thick walls and low ceilings added to the dizzying feeling you get from moving through darkness. The lady in front of me, the youngest of the group, could not keep up. She slowed, stumbled, stopped to catch her breath and so fell ever farther behind. I did not dare pass her or urge her to pick up her pace; instead, I hailed the others and asked them to slow down. But my voice must not have reached them, for they did not respond. I offered my arm to the lady and encouraged her to persevere, believing our guide would wait for us farther on, or that we would encounter someone to guide us back to the consul's apartments. But we did not meet a living soul. Guided by a faint light, we arrived on a blind terrace. Without realizing it, we must have taken a wrong turn. There was no choice but to retrace our steps. As I was about to turn around, my companion stopped me.

"When you are lost, it is better to stop, and not move, instead of becoming even more lost," she said, sitting down on the parapet. "If we stay exactly where we are, they will find us all the more readily."

From the terrace we could see the Muscat seafront and the sultan's palace. I would have liked to enjoy this brief moment of respite to admire the sea, which gleamed in the sunlight like tortoiseshell, but all I could think of was returning to the stifling entrails of the citadel. It was neither anxiety nor impatience that drove me, but the malaise caused by the presence of the young missionary. At first I thought her smile was the reason for my discomfort – more like a grimace, split in the very middle by a scar that lifted her upper lip and gave it the cutting aspect of a turtle's beak ready to grab on to your finger. I would have gladly lent myself to such a possibility had it not been for her penetrating gaze: a scrutinizing gaze impossible to bear, that fixed itself upon you and would not let you go. Not even for the blink of an eye. I soon understood why: the missionary never blinked. Her irises were of an acidic ocher hue, with yellow tinges. I suspected she was suffering from acute jaundice, for the whites of her eyes were also the color of bile – a vile, nausea-inducing shade. I am not the kind of person who believes in the evil eye, but right then, I would not have refused a protective amulet, like the blue glass *nazar* worn by the Turks, or the phalloform *fascinum* of the Romans, both with the power to deflect the attention of witches.

To steady my nerves, I began to examine the varnished tiles of the terrace floor. I could not help but point out that they resembled, in their octagonal form and amber-tinted marbling, the pattern of a turtle shell.

"Have you found in Muscat what you were seeking?" the missionary asked.

"There is no finer tortoiseshell in the world than what I have in my bags," I answered, sure of myself. "It is as light as the honey from the jujube blossom."

"There is a color even lighter than that," she said, bringing her face close to mine.

For a moment I was afraid she was referring to her eyes, and was expecting me to pay her a compliment. Instead, she wanted to draw my attention to her pince-nez, so discreet I scarcely noticed it. Attached to her ear with a fine gold chain, it was no different from those fashionable at the time, except for its frame. When I looked closer, I saw it was made of tortoise-shell, though transparent as glass and of a tint one observes only in the finest gold.

"Where did you purchase that pince-nez?" I asked, holding myself back so as not to touch it.

"I had it made by an eyeglass maker in Damascus."

"Would you know where he procured such extraordinary tortoiseshell?"

"Of course!" she answered, with a dry laugh that made her split lip rattle. "I provided it myself, and you will never guess where it comes from ..."

Just as she was about to reveal her secret, she was interrupted by the voice of our guide who had set out to find us after realizing we had disappeared. My best efforts to continue the conversation with her were sabotaged by her coreligionists, who clustered around her as soon as they saw her, and the consul, who dominated her attention for the remainder of the afternoon with his continuous warnings against heatstroke. I scarcely had time to bid her good-bye, but I did use those few moments to try to find out where she was living in Muscat. I received only the vaguest of indications.

"Our villa is near the city gates," she said, "at the edge of a date plantation where I go to meditate each morning at dawn."

I proved to be bad company for Salem that evening. When I returned, I threw only the most cursory of glances at the slices of tortoiseshell he had removed from the last carapaces, whereas normally I would have examined them one by one. To tell the truth, I had suddenly lost interest in the hawksbill shell; it now seemed too dark and of inferior quality. How had I come to despise what only a few hours earlier I so admired? I suppose that the value we attach to an object is established by way of comparison; the arrival of a rarer curiosity is enough to reduce it irremediably in our eyes. Whatever the case, I could think of nothing but how I might contrive to lay hands on a shipment of golden tortoiseshell.

"You seem preoccupied, friend," said Salem with deferential familiarity. "Now that hot weather has come, the Muscat sun must be affecting you. It is high time for you to return to your country. Take my advice, and avoid going out in the noonday sun."

I paid no heed to his words, wise though they most certainly were. The next day, upon waking, I set out toward Wadi al-Kabir, on whose banks grew the town's only date grove, reputed for producing more than sixty varieties of dates. Luck smiled upon me: I arrived just as the missionaries were emerging from a traditional dwelling with white-and-ocher stucco. In two rows, each holding a Bible, they were probably going off to preach in the desert, considering that it was forbidden, on pain of death, to proselytize among the Moslems. I was about to approach them when I realized that the lady with the pince-nez was not there. Not wanting to explain my presence, I hid in an alleyway and waited until they left before knocking at the villa door. I had barely touched the heavy bronze knocker when an Indian manservant answered. In his approximate English, he told me the young lady had already departed for the palm grove. I followed his directions and soon found myself in a plantation that bore no resemblance to our orchards. Here, the trees had not been planted in quincunx, but grew in close ranks, their dizzying height compensating for the thinness of their trunks. As agile as monkeys, young boys climbed them to fertilize the date flowers by hand, for without their precious assistance, the palms would be almost as sterile as the arid sands in which they grew. I paused to watch them as they swung from the top of the trees, then I went looking for the missionary, cautiously stepping over the many irrigation canals dug between the trees. She was seated in direct sunlight, on the rough-hewn edge of a well, eyes closed behind her pince-nez framed with tortoise-shell that gleamed even more golden in the morning sunlight. Unwilling to interrupt her meditation, I leaned against a palm's rough trunk and kept still. When at last she lifted her head, she flashed a derisive smile when she saw me waiting.

"Don't tell me you've lost your way again, and are waiting to be found," she said.

Though her joking may have been clever, I was in no mood to appreciate it. Putting pleasantries aside, I came straight to the point and laid before her the sole reason I was here: to discover what species of turtle the golden shell came from, and on what shores it could be hunted. The missionary removed her pince-nez and gave me an inquisitive look.

"You have understood only what you wished to," she said. "Who said anything about tortoiseshell?"

"What other animal produces a more delicate substance?

You are certainly not going to tell me that your pince-nez is made of fish or reptile scales ..."

"Of course not. My scales are infinitely more precious. Can't you guess?" And leaning toward me, she whispered, "They are of human origin."

Herr Linke told me that certain dishonest marquetry artists inlaid fragments of fingernails in jewel boxes or chess pieces and passed them off as ivory, and that a Bulgarian prince had acquired a reputation for cruelty by sitting on a throne carved from pinewood and inlaid with fingernails torn from the hands of his enemies. Yet not even the yellowest of nails, polished by the most skillful artisan, could ever achieve the luster of tortoiseshell, even less so the golden scales of her pince-nez. She was mocking me, I objected, and I urged her to tell the truth. She motioned to me to be patient and lifted her nose toward the sky. The wind, which only a moment earlier had been tossing the palm fronds, suddenly fell silent. Every sound of the date grove ceased, from the chirping of the birds to the burbling of the water in the irrigation ditches. The thin veil of coolness left by the night evaporated, and the heat crept into the very shade, becoming insupportable. Yet the missionary remained in sunlight. She stared at the fiery globe with eyes wide open, without blinking at all. Was she trying to blind herself? Her pupils seemed on the verge of bursting into flame. Soon, only two lumps of burnt coal would stand where her eyes once were! I could not allow the young lady to mutilate herself; I leapt forward to act as a screen between the sun and her eyes.

One of my weaknesses, Father, is my inability to see a woman cry without immediately wanting to console her. Imagine my desire when I saw big tears flowing down her cheeks. I pulled out my handkerchief and came near to dry them. But instead of moistening the fabric, they cascaded onto the lip of the well with the tinkling of small coins. Emotion gripped my throat, but I managed to cry out to her.

"Scales! They're flowing from your eyes!"

That was no exaggeration. Her lachrymal glands were secreting a substance that solidified when exposed to sunlight, and formed scaly tears. The young woman, for whom nothing could have been more natural, responded to my surprise by essaying a smile with her split lip.

"Don't be so astonished," she said. "My case is not without precedent."

And she reminded me that, in the Book of Acts, when Saint Paul converted on the road to Damascus, "there fell from his eyes as it had been scales."

Could a divine miracle be compared to the phenomenon I had just witnessed? I was tempted to believe so, since her golden tears were of immaculate purity and heavenly lightness.

"You have been in Damascus recently," I said. "Is what happened to you the result of conversion?"

"The opposite is true," she answered. "I converted when I began to see the world through scales. But the price to pay is high. Each time I look directly at the sun, my sight grows weaker. I can no longer do without my pince-nez. You can see how constant use has damaged it. One of the nose supports has come loose."

Despite my compassion for her, I could not stop myself from coveting her tears.

"Though I don't want to boast," I said, "no one could better repair your frames than I. I'll surpass that: I'll add beveling that will capture the light, and buff the surface to make them shine even more brilliantly. In exchange, I ask only for a few of your precious scales."

Her response overjoyed me.

"Take these," she said. "You will need them. If you return my pince-nez here, before sundown, I will give you all the tears I shed today."

I gathered the still-burning scales with infinite care. There was not a second to lose; I returned to Salem's house and set about repairing the pince-nez. I soon discovered that human scales were far more difficult to work than tortoiseshell. The latter can be cut like glass, with a diamond blade, and joined together without glue. By one of those mysteries of alchemy found only in nature, its plates bind to one another when subjected to heat. Human scales, on the other hand, can be cut only with the teeth. They soften sufficiently only through body heat and can be joined only with perspiration. What's more, it proved impossible to polish them with anything other than my skin. It took me six full hours to complete a minor repair, but the result was worth the effort: it could not be detected.

The sun was sinking in the sky when I returned to the palm grove. As she had promised, the missionary was waiting for me at the well. Her features were drawn and her eyes more yellow than before. She must have wept all day long, for on the lip of the well lay a substantial heap of scales. My heart full of pride,

I presented her with the pince-nez. She examined it and, to show her gratitude, pointed to the scaly tears.

"Take them," she said wearily. "Take them all."

There were enough not only to fill my pockets, but also the inside of my hat. With feverish greed, and no consideration for the missionary's state of exhaustion, I proposed yet another arrangement.

"Would you have a fan or a tortoiseshell comb that needs repairing? I would gladly make you some hairpins in exchange for a little more of this precious material."

"You will have to settle for what you have," she said. "You will not be seeing me again. We are leaving Muscat tomorrow. The Omanis are hardly promising candidates for conversion."

I was about to insist, but the intensity of her gaze froze me. At least I would not have to confront her again, I thought, some consolation for my disappointment. I turned to her one final time before leaving the palm grove. In the gathering darkness of evening, I saw two yellowish lights that flickered like the will-o'-the-wisps that draw lost travelers into the swamp. A shiver ran down my spine, and I moved on, certain I had narrowly avoided going even more astray.

My ship would not be sailing for another week, so I busied myself joining all the scales into a single plaque – which cost me no small amount of effort. The task was as complex as inlaying the cupola of a mosque with mosaic tiles, and made no easier by Salem's frequent interruptions. He had been harassing me ever since I made the mistake of telling him about my adventure.

"You have been bewitched by a jinn," he said, "a demon made of subtle, smokeless flame that assumes a human form to make men stray from piety. The Prophet also once met a woman with yellow eyes. He declared she possessed the evil eye and ordered that she be exorcized. These scales are devilish – you must burn them!"

Unlike Salem, I was convinced that the missionary's tears were inoffensive. Not only did I have no reason to get rid of them, I fully intended to sell them to the highest bidder during my stopover in London. I hoped to turn a handsome profit, perhaps enough to set myself up in business. To tell the whole truth, Father, I was haunted by a thought that, ever since it came to me, took shape in my mind with such vigor that it could not be extirpated, as bizarre as it was. Curiosity tormented me: what would the world look like through the golden filter of her tears? Like the missionary, would I, too, experience an epiphany that would lead me to apostleship? On the eve of my departure, I locked myself in my room and sat down in front of the mirror. Holding my eyelids open with my thumb and forefinger, I placed a scale on each cornea. At first I screamed with pain, for the scale burned like pepper. But once I grew accustomed to its heat, I saw in the looking glass that my yellow eyes had taken on a frozen, fixed gaze. I myself was intimidated. Immediately I thought of the many advantages they offered should I need to assert myself. What bully would now dare to importune me? To put my newfound authority to the test, I went for a stroll along the seafront, where the inhabitants of Muscat would congregate for a promenade at sunset, after the cannon shot announced the closing of the city gates. As I went past men clothed in white robes, women concealed behind their leather masks and undisciplined children running every which way, shouting at the top of their voices, I made another discovery. More than my appearance, it was the way I looked upon my fellow human beings that had changed. I was struck by how petty and ridiculous they looked, how mediocre. The yellow of the scales accentuated all faults, emphasized malformations and infirmities. I had never seen so many hunchbacks, crooked noses, malformed members and twisted mouths, peeling skin and eruptions of pustules, limping legs and curved spines. Humanity suddenly seemed hideous and repulsive. For the first time, I beheld the world in all its irremediable ugliness. How could anyone tolerate the presence of a nature so monstrous, whose issue was so imperfect, abnormal and degenerate? I wasn't surprised that the young missionary wept so copiously as she contemplated it. Disgust for life threw me into such despair I could not even measure its depths. Salem was right. The scales gave me the evil eye and were leading me toward the abyss. Like Saint Paul, it was high time they fell from my eyes.

It never occurred to me that I might have trouble getting rid of them. Imagine my anguish when I realized they were stuck to my corneas. I ran along the beach, crushing the remains of baby turtles that had been devoured by crabs and foxes, and thrust my face into the sea in hopes that salt water would unfasten the scales. Instead, it strengthened the bond. I tried to pull them off with my fingernails but succeeded only in drawing blood. I had to face the facts: I was now forced to see the world in its most horrific light. I could not even avert my eyes, for my lids would no longer shut.

In that state, I began the journey home. The ship's doctor examined me, but could do nothing. For endless days, I wandered the deck, disgusted by the bilious sky and the brownish, miasmic swells. Finally I reached the only possible conclusion: I preferred blindness to living this way.

There are some things that the most unbending will cannot impose upon the body without it revolting and asserting its rights: to stop breathing for more than a few moments, to remain awake for more than a few days, to repress a hiccough or the urge to regurgitate when the uvula is tickled ... Just as it is impossible to keep the pupil from contracting when it is exposed to light, you cannot force your eyes to stare directly at the sun without blinking. A time comes when the eyelids clamp shut and the head turns away with the violence of a drowning man fighting for life. I am proud to say I am made of stronger stuff. I did not hesitate when the sun's piercing rays burned my retinas. And I kept my head raised to the heavens even after I had been thrown forever into darkness.

Be in no hurry to grant me pardon, Father, for I have not completed my confession. The worst is yet to come. I must tell you, in my own defense, that I absolutely refused to sell the plaque I made from the missionary's tears. But by a slip of the hand imputable to my blindness, it fell among the light-hued tortoiseshell I delivered to Parker's. When I discovered my error, it was too late to recover it. Just this morning, I learned Herr Linke used it to repair the frames of your eyeglasses. Yes, the very ones you are wearing on your nose. I can make out their pale yellow light through the shadowy darkness I now inhabit. I could have sworn, Father, that two jinns were drawing me into the swamps of Hell.

CORONA SUPPLICIORUM

FORGIVE ME, FATHER, if I keep my gloves on while confessing. I prefer not to touch this armrest contaminated by so many sin-stained fingers, for is it not true that what soils the hands also soils the soul? I know that only prelates are allowed to wear gloves inside the church but, as you can see, the gloves I am wearing have nothing in common with those embroidered gold- and pearl-stitched objects of vanity affected by kings even unto their tombs. These are not made of chamois or goatskin, nor have they enjoyed, like Beau Brummell's, the attentions of three glove makers: one for the fingers, one for the palms and one for the cuffs. Mine are humble gardening gloves, similar to those worn by rose lovers since antiquity. You may well need such gloves yourself, Father. Only a few moments ago I saw you holding in your bare hands a rose that an anonymous lady of our parish left on your altar. You may have wounded your finger, and who knows in what purulent infection such a puncture might result?

Does not the Bible tell us that thorns and thistles grow only on earth? Which means there were no roses in the Garden of Eden. Only trees bearing edible fruits, and a few groves where Adam and Eve concealed their nudity. In my opinion, this so-called garden, with its four quadrants separated by the four forks of a river, better warrants the name of orchard. You may think me blasphemous, but it seems to me that man, with the sweat of his brow and without the assistance of a superior power, has succeeded in creating on earth places far more worthy of the word "paradise." I do not mean English gardens, or those flower beds that so delight the French, or those Italian follies where domesticated nature reminds me of a waiting room for souls in Purgatory. No, the gardens of earthy delights to which I allude are those designed by the Persians to provide pious Moslems with a foretaste of the afterlife.

I myself have seen the gardens of Shiraz, and let me assure you that nothing is more miraculous, in the midst of those arid plains, than the green sanctuaries where shade and freshness are cultivated above all else. Their design, always rectangular, is set out by an edge of sycamores, myrtle and fruit trees; if you are walking there, you need only reach out your hand and pluck a honeyed fig or a juicy apricot. Within the garden stretches a mosaic of flower beds, with spandrels of lilacs and arabesques of zinnias, tulips, irises and carnations. The pathways converge on the central basin, where elaborate decorations of blue faience tiles mingle with the reflection of the pleasure pavilion under a mass of roses. These gardens attained such perfection that they inspired the ornamental motifs of the magnificent carpets woven under the Sasanid, Samanid and Safavid dynasties. The first carpet mentioned in Persian literature is a fabulous work representing the gardens of the great palace of Ctesiphon, with its ruby- and emerald-incrusted flowers, which was presented to the Shah Chosroes so that he might have something to contemplate during the winter months.

I must tell you, Father, that for more than thirty years I have collected Persian carpets. I inherited this passion from my mother, for whom furniture, draperies and *objets d'art* were no more than accessories designed to complement and display the richly woven handiwork that covered the hardwood floors. She firmly believed that there was no finer criterion for evaluating people's taste, the breadth of their culture and the depth of their emotions than their interest in her carpets. Whoever proved so unfortunate as to walk on them without showing respect never received a second invitation. Early on, I learned to take off my shoes when I entered the house, and walk across the carpets in a random manner to avoid undue wear and to step over their fringes without disturbing them. To pass the time on rainy days, my mother would challenge me to identify the various decorative motifs that she pointed at with her toe: the stylized tear that is called *boteh*, the octagonal *gol* also known as the "elephant's foot," the *berati* rosette, the *zil-e sultan* vase flanked by a bird and the tree of life. At age thirteen, I knew the difference between a Tabriz and a Kashan, between a Kerman and a Ferahan. At twenty, by touching the back of a carpet I could determine its density – no small achievement when you know that a carpet worthy of the name may number more than 350 knots per square inch.

I was very attached to my mother. Often I would accompany her to the dressmaker's, and spend hours coiffing her magnificent mahogany hair. I was twenty when she died after a bad fall from a horse. To recover from this cruel loss, I sold off her collection of thirty-two carpets and wagered all my gains on a piece of inexpressible beauty found in a private auction: a Khorasan carpet similar to the one depicted in Vermeer's *The Music Lesson*. I laid it on the sofa in my living room, where it was always within close reach. But the consolation it brought me was short-lived. Within a few weeks, I tired of its rough texture, and was considering replacing it with a silken Isfahan prayer rug that had caught my eye in the show window of the official supplier to the railway magnates of Montreal, and on which I had cast a covetous eye after simply running a finger across its surface. But once I captured the piece, for all its exceptional softness, my affection strayed, and I almost immediately traded it for a Senneh carpet woven during the reign of Shah Abbas the Great, depicting a boar-hunting scene. The coats of the animals were so superbly imitated that I shivered as I stroked them.

I could have covered the floors of ten houses with the carpets that have passed through my hands, and assumed my rightful place among the great collectors. But it is not in my nature to accumulate. You may accuse me of frivolity, but I never grow too fond of anything, and never hesitate to let go what belongs to me, the better to pursue what is not yet mine. So it was, from one conquest to another, through a series of judicious transactions that each earned me a fabulous profit. Last year I became the owner of what many experts consider the world's rarest carpet: the celebrated Star of Ardabil, which owes its surname to the constellations decorating its border. Its indigo field strewn with pearly flowers depicts a garden by moonlight. The first time I touched it, I nearly fainted, so dense and close-knit was its velvet surface. Imagine! That carpet contained not less than thirty-two million knots – a colossal amount of work, even for a master capable of tying ten thousand knots a day! According to legend, it had been the most precious adornment of the Jannat Sara, the House of Paradise built next to the mausoleum of Sheikh Safi al-Din, in Ardabil. It is said the Russians stole it in 1827, when they sacked the town. Whatever the case, I acquired it through the good offices of the highly reputed Viennese merchant Siegler. Herr Karl, the proprietor, had been one of the first to begin importing after the Vienna International Exposition had reawakened European interest in Oriental carpets some thirty years earlier. No one knew Persia better than he. He crossed the Elburz peaks and the mountains of Zagros in search of the most beautiful pieces woven by nomadic tribes. He brought back, from the Qashqai region, a carpet made of unspun wool as fine as silk, in red and blue hues of exceptional intensity, which he later sold to the well-known neurologist Sigmund Freud, and which now covered the couch in his consulting room. If anyone could appreciate the worth of the Ardabil carpet, Herr Karl was that person – and he made me pay accordingly.

"Next time," I told him upon completing the transaction, "I will have no choice but to turn all Persia upside down to find a carpet that gives me such intense emotion."

Herr Karl nodded as if in agreement. Then, after a moment of hesitation, he changed his mind.

"Unless, of course, you should make your way to Shiraz …"

"What could I hope to accomplish in Shiraz?" I asked, unable to conceal my surprise. "Its carpet weavers are skilled, but their work cannot compare with this Ardabil."

"On my trip to that city, the head of the master weavers' guild told me that in one of the palaces could be found a carpet hardly larger than a prayer mat, woven by a single artisan, numbering no fewer than forty million knots."

"Hardly believable! The man must have devoted his life to it!"

"I did not see the object itself," Herr Karl admitted. "It may only be a rumor."

I don't know if the Viennese merchant spoke those words to dampen my ardor, but they had quite the opposite effect.

I immediately lost all interest in the Ardabil Star. Once I returned to my hotel room, I did not even bother to unroll it; I packed it away in my trunk and prepared my luggage. The next day, I departed for Istanbul on the Orient Express. From there, neither the jolting of the Ottoman railways nor the ambushes along the Persian roads could stop me from reaching Shiraz. At the time, Shah Mozaffar od-Din had just ascended the throne of his assassinated father, and within a matter of months he had brought his realm to the verge of bankruptcy by borrowing immense sums from the Russians and the French to finance his official visits to the capitals of Europe. His creditors, meanwhile, laid hands on the mining concessions and infiltrated the highest spheres of influence. When I arrived there, Shiraz was lousy with foreigners scheming for control of the trade route to the Persian Gulf for the export of opium, tobacco and cotton to the outposts of Port Said and Bombay. In the Vakil Bazaar, petty merchants sold slippers and spices for a king's ransom. As for the carpet sellers, they didn't think twice about passing on carpets tinted with artificial dyes to naive buyers, though the government had formally forbidden the use of such substances. The head of the guild, Sheikh Arash Borhani, deplored the decline in quality at length when I met him in the alcove he occupied in the heart of the bazaar. He approved only of dyes derived from walnut shells, vine leaves, pomegranate peel and azurite.

"In olden days," he said, pouring me a glass of rose-petal tea, "when Shiraz was the capital of Persia, the finest carpets woven in the nearby mountains were not for foreign eyes. They were reserved for the Shah's exclusive use. All were sent to Tehran when the court moved there, with one sole exception, and that one is now owned by our governor. It is called Eram, the Carpet of Paradise."

Sheikh Borhani confirmed it was none other than the legendary carpet of forty million knots, the one he had praised to Herr Karl. I begged Borhani to introduce me to the governor.

"You need no introduction to meet him," he said. "As a foreigner, you are quite naturally welcome at the receptions he gives each afternoon in his gardens. If he learns you are a carpet fancier, he will certainly show you the Eram, for he is inordinately proud of it."

I was rather surprised to hear that one could maintain a garden in such an arid climate, but I soon discovered that Shiraz was blessed with an extensive system of underground canals that brought water down from the mountains to irrigate even the smallest parcel of land. In fact, the city was so rich in gardens and vineyards, it had acquired the title of City of Wine and Roses, delicacies abundantly praised by the poets Hafez and Sa'di, both of whom were natives of Shiraz. Since I was already late, I lost no time and hurried to the palace of Eram, the governor's residence by royal prerogative. The two guards posted at the gates bowed obsequiously and ushered me in. I followed a pathway bordered by cypress and soon reached a pool of clear water where the mirror image of the spiral columns of the palace was reflected, whose moldings were as appetizing as a pastry-shop window. Among the flower beds, beneath the shade of venerable almond trees, strolled the governor's guests: British attachés, a Russian delegation, an Italian count, an Ottoman ambassador and countless French envoys whose perorations drowned out the singing nightingales. The air was heavy with the perfume the roses had captured among the folds of their lip-like petals, and now were shamelessly exhaling. As I bent over, better to smell them, from behind me I heard a bleating voice.

"There are two kinds of gardeners: those who love roses, and the rest. I hope you are not one of the rest."

The man who had spoken to me was an Anglican priest, and the founder of the Sussex Horticultural Society. He had come to Shiraz at the invitation of the governor, who had requested that he create a blue rose that would bear the name of Shah Mozaffar, and would be presented to the sovereign on his birthday. Reverend Baxter was accompanied by a young woman whom he introduced as his assistant, and who herself looked like a rosebush, for she wore countless flowers on her head in the form of crown. To complete the picture, her hair was the color of rosewood, and fell to her waist – not in silky, supple curls, but like a brambly, bushy thicket. It was like an enclosure of thorny shrubs protecting the castle of a sleeping beauty, ready to ensnare in its net any hand that might stray. Her coiffure gave the lady a severe appearance that was not helped by a defect in her upper lip, a kind of dart-shaped scar. The scar twisted itself into a disapproving frown when I told the reverend I had little interest in gardens, be they roses or anything else, and that my sole passion was Persian carpets.

"What is a Persian carpet if not a poor, reduced, artificial substitute for a garden?" she asked scornfully. "No one can appreciate the beauty of the former without understanding the art of the latter. Fortunately, you could not have come to a better place to begin your education, for this is the most beautiful of all the gardens of Shiraz. It is called the *Bagh-e Eram*, the Garden of Paradise."

"You may well be right," I replied, irritated. "But the carpet has a clear advantage over the garden: it is a bit of paradise one can own. And I fully intend to convince the governor to sell me his."

When he heard that, Reverend Baxter hastened to caution me.

"The Eram carpet is the apple of the governor's eye! He will never agree to sell it."

"At best, he will propose a wager," added his assistant. "But be warned. He is a trickster who will make you lose all you hold dear."

Scoffing at her wise advice, I went to meet the master of the place, an amiable gentleman wearing an extravagantly embellished pair of satin gloves. When he learned I was the owner of the Ardabil Star, he was more than delighted to show me his paradise carpet.

"We must hurry if we want to take advantage of the day's last light," he said as he led me up the staircase to the palace terrace.

From that vantage point, I looked down on the garden that lay at my feet. Despite the gathering darkness, I could not deny that the reverend's assistant had been telling the truth: Eram or Eden, the garden was indeed a vast natural carpet with its central medallion, its border, its fringes. The governor clapped his hands, and immediately his servants lit hundreds of perforated lamps set around the reflecting pool and along the footpaths. The water put on a robe of lunar silk and the flowers, in their beds, shone like tarnished vermilion. For a moment I felt I was standing before my Ardabil. This wonder was only a foretaste of what awaited me in the salon into which the governor showed me. The room, which opened onto the terrace, was lined with pieces of mirror in which the twilight's orange hues broke into glittering sequins that illuminated what could have easily passed for a magic carpet from a Persian fairy tale. The design depicted a luxuriant garden, with thick bushes and espaliers of climbing roses. Each flower was knit with such precision that it was possible to count the leaves, stems and even the thorns. On the lips of the petals, dewdrops seemed to scintillate in the sun. A profusion of gold threads lent it the translucent brilliance of fine enamel.

"Stroke its velvet," the governor urged me. "It is as delicate as the secret petals of a virgin ..."

But I did not dare touch it, Father. My whole life, I dreamed only of possession; now, for the first time, I wanted to give myself entirely. Yes, give myself to the Carpet of Paradise! So powerful was my veneration that I felt myself falling into idolatry. Unable to contain my feelings of adoration, I threw myself to the ground in ecstasy.

The governor seized my moment of weakness to make me the most deceitful of propositions.

"Give me your Ardabil," he said. "In exchange, you will have the chance to win the Eram."

I risked being defrauded, but the glimmer of faint hope was enough to convince me to accept the governor's conditions. With no further negotiations, I handed my treasure to him.

"Well met!" he said, rubbing his hands. "And now I challenge you to guess the exact number of colors my carpet contains. Since I am a magnanimous fellow, I will give you until tomorrow at midday to consider it."

Resolving such a riddle should have been child's play for me. But the Eram carpet was a mirage of indefinable reflections. The tips of its protruding threads, you see, had not been dyed. The artist who knotted them had patiently matched the infinite variations in tone of natural wool, which he must have chosen with circumspection from lambs, goats, camels and I know not what other animals. The browns, the rust colors and the lighter tones seemed to multiply in countless shimmering hues. Even the whites and the blacks were not constant. I spent the night trying to decide. At times I was convinced that the carpet had no more than five colors. An instant later, I would have sworn it featured more than a thousand. At dawn, I went to meditate on the matter in the rose garden of the Sa'di mausoleum. Young men stretched out in the shade of the cypress were reciting the poet's verses while, at the far ends of the pathways, gardeners were busy reorganizing great masses of potted bougainvillea, a task carried out daily to give the garden an ever-changing aspect. The brilliance of the purple, magenta and orange flowers, the sweet smell of roses, the lilting song of the nightingales combined to compose a poem that made the weight of my cares even heavier. As I strolled past the teahouse where men were quietly smoking their narghiles, I recognized Reverend Baxter's assistant by her exuberant coiffure. She was seated at a table in front of a cup of pomegranate sorbet. I greeted her from a distance, and she was kind enough to beckon me to join her. I was eager to tell her about the Eram carpet, but felt it more politic to first inquire as to the hybridization of the blue rose. Apparently, the reverend had succeeded in coaxing forth one blossom of a timid, Parma-blue color, but he had not lost faith. The Sa'di rose garden contained seventy-two varieties and he was determined to crossbreed all of them.

"Maybe it would be more useful," I ventured, "to try to make a rose without thorns ..."

Unbeknownst to me, by that remark I had proven my ignorance. I was put straightaway in my place.

"Roses have no thorns," my tablemate declared. "They have
prickles! Thorns are sharply pointed shoots that cannot be
torn off without injuring the plant. Prickles, on the other hand,
are just stuck to the stem and can be easily removed. Their
forms are as varied as the petals of a rose: some resemble teeth,
others hooks, still others, the hairs of nettles. Which means
that here, there are at least seventy-two ways of pricking your
finger. Didn't you notice the fine examples of prickles in the
Eram carpet?"

I took that opportunity to complain to the young woman
that I would not, in all probability, have another chance to
admire the Carpet of Paradise, for I could not determine how
many colors it contained. She cast me a reproving glance.

"What a fine mess you're in! Didn't I warn you about the
governor's deviousness? If you had listened to me, you would
still be in possession of your Ardabil Star. Fortunately for you,
I have a sharp ear, and I can help you."

She told me their host appreciated the wine of Shiraz to
excess. One evening, she came upon him in the hall of mirrors,
lying on his carpet, murmuring, "How soft is your fleece, my
seventy-two *houris* of Paradise!" At the time, she paid no heed
to the ramblings of that drunkard.

"Now that I think of it again, I suspect that the Eram may
well be knit from the hair of seventy-two virgins ..."

When I heard those words, I leapt to my feet. I promised
the young lady my undying gratitude, excused myself for

taking leave of her in such a cavalier fashion and rushed out of the Sa'di rose garden. A carpet woven from women's hair! If I'd only had the audacity to touch it, I would have immediately recognized the human origin of tufts so fine, and never made the gross error of mistaking them for ordinary animal hair! I presented myself at the governor's palace without bothering to shave. Once again, I was led into the hall of mirrors where the sun shone brilliantly through every aperture. A single glance was enough to prove that the young woman had not been wrong: the colors of the carpet corresponded to those of human hair. Whether or not they came from true virgins was fortunately not a question I was required to solve. I took care not to tip my hand to the governor, and put on my most pitiable expression to inform him I had abandoned the wager. I had not succeeded in finding the answer to his question and was reduced to guesswork.

"Of course, of course, my dear friend," he said with a broad smile. "Give a number, any number."

I shook my head, shifted my weight from one foot to another and pretended to count on my fingers. After endless hesitation, in a clarion voice, I announced the result.

"Seventy-two!"

The governor blanched. Letting out low, moaning sounds, he began to gnaw at his fist. I gave him no time to recover from his defeat; I rolled up the Eram, placed it on my shoulder and left the palace without further ado.

Returning to my room, I unrolled the carpet on my bed. Lying on the pillows, it looked like a sleeping woman. I spent the afternoon contemplating the beauties of its rose garden of delights. At sundown, I began to draw closer, gently approaching it, brushing against it casually. I rolled part of its fringe around my index finger, then my hands crept up its sleek flank. I hoped to excite its senses, and bring forth a shiver. My more insistent caresses finally drew a sigh from it. Then I bent over and let my hands stray across it in all directions, discovering one by one the seventy-two crowning glories that, in my mind, resembled pubic fleece. All the while, my nails tried to penetrate their deepest reaches, but they were knitted too tightly; the velvet was more tightly closed than a hymen. I did not press the issue. I would be patient, and the virgins of paradise would open their mysteries. After years of vain wandering, I had finally found the carpet of my life. Sealing my engagement with a kiss, I swore it love, respect and fidelity.

I could not have departed Shiraz without thanking the young lady with the flowering hair. In search of the most precious gift, I returned to Sheikh Arash Borhani's stall at the Vakil Bazaar to ask his counsel. He showed me a turquoise inlaid saddle pommel, a shawl so finely woven that it could pass through a ring, a bottle of rose water of the same quality used for the semiannual laving of the Ka'bah in Mecca. But he had better still: a flask of blown glass containing rose essence, the most precious of all perfumes, each ounce the result of the distillation of ten thousand flowers, worth thrice its weight in gold. That was what I presented Reverend Baxter's assistant when I next saw her in the Sa'di rose garden. My gift pleased her so well that she promptly sprinkled some on her tresses. Her movement disturbed her coiffure, and one of the pins that held it in place fell to the ground. I hastened to pick it up, and was startled to see that it was a long, extremely sharp needle.

"My mother's hairpins were prudently blunted," I said. "This one could injure you."

"It is not a pin," the young woman replied. "It is a prickle!"

I was a little bewildered; must she compare everything to roses? I suggested I could help her with her coiffure. As I had long ago done with my mother, I stood behind her and began by running my hands through her hair whose rosewood hue would have nicely embellished the Carpet of Paradise. But hardly had I thrust my fingers into her curls when the shooting pain of a thousand needles stabbed my palms. Just imagine, Father! The hair on her head bristled with dangerously sharpened thorns that grew from her scalp with astonishing vigor.

"You have a crown of thorns!" I cried, drawing back my fingers thick with blood. "How is that possible?"

"Not thorns," she replied, discouragement in her voice. "Prickles!"

Those thorns – or prickles – must have had irritating properties, for no sooner had I taken leave of the young woman than my hands began to swell, and soon were so engorged I could feel the throbbing of my pulse. I went back to my room and soaked them in water. But I felt only revulsion. In the cool water that appeared perfectly clear and undisturbed, I felt I was brushing long ribbons of tangled algae. I stirred the liquid mass, and had the feeling of squelching through a magma of gluey leaves in which I came across decomposing rhizomes and all sorts of marsh plants in a stage of decomposition. I attributed those hallucinations of the skin to the edema that affected my hands, and tried to reassure myself. The sensation would slowly disappear as the inflammation eased. But the hypersensibility only increased and, after several more days, every smooth surface seemed riddled with texture. I could not run my fingers over a polished stone or across a lacquered piece of furniture without touching, with painful acuity, something that felt like coarse bark, bare twigs, petals gnawed by insects, stems turgid with canker. It was as though some infernal sculptor had found perverse pleasure in gouging vegetable horrors into the surface of the world.

In this condition, I could not even touch the Eram carpet, and I began to miss it cruelly. I tried sliding the back of my hand across it, but the pleasure was not the same as when I stroked it with my fingers. Then came a time when the temptation was too great and, the better to succumb to it without remorse, I told myself that the Carpet of Paradise would contribute to my healing. What folly! I placed my diseased palms upon it. Immediately I felt that several wiry hairs stuck out from its velvet surface, making it rough, almost coarse to the touch. Frustrated in the extreme, I fetched my razor and meticulously evened the surface. As I worked, my hands discovered that the carpet was not as unblemished as it had first appeared. It was covered with asperities that were plainly not accidents attributable to the clumsiness of the weaver, but motifs quite purposely sculpted out in bas-relief, forming a hidden image that could be sensed only by the most attentive palpations. This secret image had nothing in common with the eye-pleasing motifs of the rose garden. No, its border represented a field of couch grass and darnel writhing with snakes and pustulent toads; fingers that strayed there would be wounded by clumps of sharp-edged plantain, and would barely be able to hack a path through the spiny thistle bracts. I sought out the seventy-two virgins in this garden of torments and found them imprisoned in bramblebushes. Bound by creeping lianas, blindfolded by nettles, they cried out their pain through their viney gags. I took up my razor and, with brutal strokes, cut them free. In my feverish excitement, I did not realize I had shaved the entire carpet to the weft.

If I cannot do without my gloves, it is because I have never been able to rid myself of the hypersensitivity that has caused me to disbelieve in my hands. They find evil in all they touch. And when joined in prayer, they accuse each other of the most grievous obscenities. I dare not think of what they might find in the pages of the Bible or, worse yet, on the communion wafer! I would like to spare you such a fate, Father. That is why I am warning you against the roses you will find on the altar. I saw the anonymous parishioner who leaves them for you there every morning. I recognized the thorn-like scar on her lips. Soon she will come and ask that you lay your hands upon her afflicted head. Refuse her your blessing! Even if her rosewood hair attracts you. For, as you know, there are no roses without thorns. Pardon; without prickles.

OLEATUM PANDAEMONIUM

BLESS ME, FATHER, for I have sinned. I neglected to dip my fingers in the holy water as I entered the church. Not for want of desire to cross myself; quite the opposite. No one seeks the protection of the Cross more than I. But the holy water was not as clean as it should have been. An iridescent oily film floated on its surface. I can recognize that oil among a thousand. I know where it comes from and who poured it. Once I have revealed that person's identity, you will wish to incinerate your stoup.

When you saw me genuflect just now, you may well have thought, "This man may be in greater need of a wash than to be cleansed of his sins." I can hardly blame you. You scrutinize my grime-encrusted face, my greasy eyebrows, my ringworm-ravaged beard and you conclude that I am the most abject of beggars. My stench, quite unlike what you associate with saintliness, offends your nostrils. You would prefer that I leave the confessional door at least ajar to evacuate the effluvia. You must wonder how long you will be able to listen to me before having to leave the church for fresh air.

A shame that this screened peephole does not let you see all of me, for then you would realize that my body, in contrast to my face, reveals the infinite care I lavish upon it. Every morning, it is bathed, scrubbed, curried, powdered; no garment touches it unless it has been meticulously bleached, brushed and ironed. Even the nails of my fingers and toes are cleaned, filed and polished daily. Perhaps you would pay me greater heed if you knew I am the owner of the province's largest soap factory. The housewives of your parish no doubt use our Gabou soap bars, our Winnie floor-cleaning products, our Yvonne laundry flakes, sold in the best grocery stores in their distinctive boxes featuring a raccoon. And even if you have not shaved with our highly reputed Winston cream, you have certainly washed your hands with one of our popular, violet-scented Béatou soaps. We manufacture all these products in industrial quantities, using a fully automated process.

There is no use pretending that this factory hasn't made me a fortune, and won me the epithet The King of Soaps – a title that, once upon a time, I bore with a certain legitimacy for, believe it or not, I have a boyish face and naturally light skin. "Skin like a baby's bottom," my second cousin Aurelia put it. Though she is a poor relation, she boasts of a rosy complexion and skin so fine, its perfection has never been altered by the slightest blemish. My work has made me extraordinarily sensitive to other people's epidermis; that is why I am, at thirty, still a bachelor. Given my advantageous situation, I was not lacking in suitable matches. But every time a mother would present her daughter to me, my eye spied a blackhead, an angry pimple, a dilated pore that drove me away. By a process of elimination, I reached the conclusion that Aurelia would not be a bad choice, despite the inferiority of her position. A modest background can, after all, be better concealed than damaged skin … So last summer, I made up my mind to ask for her hand. I went to her boardinghouse shortly after the supper hour and was shown into the boudoir, where Aurelia was busy darning stockings. I had brought neither flowers nor candies but my hands were far from empty: I had brought with me a gift box of six bars of lily of the valley–scented soap, a new product greatly appreciated by our city's more elegant ladies. My gift, however, instead of bringing with it the effusion of gratitude I had been anticipating, created such embarrassment that I did not know where to put my feet. After a lengthy silence, Aurelia confessed that she did not use my products because they were too abrasive for her sensitive skin. Abrasive! My lanolin-enriched soaps, extracted from the most unctuous lamb suint! Never had I heard such shocking remarks, and my amour propre was stung to the quick. But my entrepreneurial spirit quickly asserted itself and, undeterred by indiscretion, I urged my second cousin to reveal the secret of her exquisite skin.

"Wait for me here," she said, getting to her feet. "I will return in a moment."

I heard her climb the stairs and walk across the floor above. When she returned, she placed before me a small packet wrapped in curious blue paper covered with Arabic letters. I unwrapped it and discovered a perfectly square bar of soap the color of old parchment, engraved with a seal depicting an olive branch. From its unctuous perfume that one instinctively associates with irreproachable cleanliness, I had no difficulty determining that I was holding in my hands an authentic cake of sabon Nabulsi, renowned throughout the world for its soft lather and great cleansing power. Only the finest connoisseur could appreciate these qualities – which convinced me that Aurelia would be an ideal wife.

"I buy it from a pharmacist on Craig Street," she explained. "I devote half my meager wage to it. I would gladly give you my hand if you assure me on your honor that I will never want for it."

Kneeling before her, I pledged her this oath.

"I shall do better than purchase it for you in great quantity. I guarantee that before our wedding day, my factory will produce as much as you desire. I swear it will pave the pathway to the altar!"

I was bold to undertake such an engagement: the formula of sabon Nabulsi is, after all, the best-kept secret of soap making. Its sole ingredients that can be identified are olive oil and *souad* – the legendary natural soda obtained by Bedouin tribesmen by burning the branches of the barilla plant found along the banks of the Jordan. Over the centuries, many have attempted – without success – to imitate it. The Crusaders, who knew nothing of soap before arriving at Nablus, threatened to level the city if its soap makers did not reveal their secret. Cleverly, they handed over the recipe used by their competitors in Aleppo, which was brought back to Europe and used in soap making in Marseille and Castille. It was clear that, if I hoped to succeed where the Crusaders had failed, I would have to undertake my own crusade, and travel to the Holy Land.

For the sake of my cousin Aurelia's lovely skin, I departed for Nablus at the end of September. It is a small town, situated at the crossroads of the routes leading from Jerusalem to the Jordan, and from Damascus to Mecca, in a fertile valley planted with olive trees, lying between Mounts Ebal and Gerizim – the sacred precinct of the Samaritans. Upon arrival, I was surprised to find not one, but thirty flourishing soap works. Symbols of wealth and prestige, they were administered by powerful clans that fought not only over the land, but the peasants, artisans, workers and traders as well. I was disappointed that I could not visit them. They were situated in veritable fortresses capable of housing hundreds of people, under guard of heavily armed men. For all that, they would frequently fall victim to arson, or witness skirmishes that inevitably degenerated into bloodbaths.

I could have rented a comfortable villa on the slopes of Mount Ebal, but I preferred to stay at the khan, the great caravansary where all merchants on their way to or from Nablus take lodgings. My room was above the stables, at the far end of an arcade that enclosed an inner courtyard where Bedouins would gather of an evening to play dominoes. I shared my modest quarters with a man from Hebron come to sell his blown-glass oil lamps, all in the same cobalt-blue shade and stored in wooden cases filled with straw, which took up much of the space between the two beds. As he unwrapped the objects, the better for me to admire them, he related how he had been apprenticed as a five-year-old to a glass workshop, under the supervision of an intransigent master who had taken two decades to award him journeyman status.

"One can learn to play the *ney* at any age," he told me. "But if you have not begun to blow glass by early childhood, you will never be able to excel in the art."

But his profession had extracted a weighty tribute from him. He suffered from a chronic cough, and the heat of the ovens had wrinkled his face so deeply, he looked twice his age. I purchased a handsome oil lamp that I did not need, but I could always give it to Aurelia.

"And you?" he asked. "What have you come looking for in this part of the world?"

When he heard that I coveted the recipe for the soap that bore the seal of the olive branch, he stared at me as though I were mad.

"Unfortunate man! The olive branch is the seal of the Jabal family whose soap manufacture supplies all Egypt and the Hejaz! Of all the clans of Nablus, they are not only the most powerful, but the most ferocious, with a reputation for disposing of their rivals by throwing them into vats of boiling soap. If you value your life, forget this senseless idea!"

Apparently, the glassblower knew of what he spoke; every time he tried to approach the Jabal family residence to sell his oil lamps, he was immediately driven away by the sentinels. I didn't want to insult him by taking his warning lightly, but I was not ready to abandon the match before it had begun, and asked him to tell me more. I learned that only the concessionaires of the major importers were admitted to the *diwan* – the family council chamber where business matters were dealt with. The information did not fall upon deaf ears. It rapidly germinated and produced a gambit that – I was sure of it – would throw open the ironclad portals of the forbidden soap maker.

The next day, I presented myself at the Jabal residence and, through the grilled peephole, pretended to be the charterer for a cargo ship anchored in Jaffa harbor that would transport to America as much soap as its hold could contain. A few moments later, under close guard, I was brought before the chief of the clan, the fearsome Hajj Nimr al-Jabal, a man with dagger-sharp features and eyes blacker than the turban that rested upon his bushy eyebrows, and who gave no appearance of wishing to negotiate. I said nothing about the price he set; I did, however, ask to examine the merchandise. The chief nodded for me to follow him through a vaulted passage leading to the soap works. When I came upon the copper vat, as large as a nuptial bed, whose contents were bubbling away above a fire stoked by shovelfuls of olive stones, I was scared stiff, fearing my end had come. But I was wrong to be concerned, for instead I enjoyed the rare privilege of visiting the premises, and I committed to memory every detail of the experience. I saw the underground containers where the olive oil is stored, and the pits in which the caustic soda is fermented. I observed how the workers, after stirring the soap mixture for eight days, poured it directly onto a broad wooden plank frame, spread it out evenly, then divided it into sections with a wire soaked in red dye. I admired the soap cutters slicing the squares and stamping them with a metal seal. In the drying chamber, where the soap is stacked in tall, open columns that resemble cakes of beeswax, I played my trump card. Drawing from my sleeve one of my famous Béatou violet-scented soaps, I proudly presented it to Hajj Nimr al-Jabal. I, too, I confessed, was a major soap producer. If he agreed to sell me his formula, I promised to market it through my factory and pay him a reasonable percentage of the profits. His reaction was not long in coming. In a harsh voice, he barked out an order in Arabic. Three of his muscular henchmen seized me and threw me into the street as if I were the most abject of beggars. To complete my humiliation, they threw the cake of soap I had brought, hitting me in the head, but not without spitting on it first! I was overcome with blind fury, and shook my fist at the watchtower that loomed over the walls.

"I shall learn your secret," I cried out as the rubberneckers in the street around me burst into laughter. "I shall make a soap far better than yours, and soon you will come crawling to plead for my formula."

I stalked off to the caravansary and, along the way, purchased a pot and caustic soda. I stopped off as well at a local olive grower who, as luck would have it, happened to be bringing in the year's harvest of the fruit of a two-thousand-year-old olive tree – a tree beneath which Christ must have sought shelter when he lived among the Samaritans! I assisted the old man in plucking the olives from the highest branches, one at a time so as not to bruise them, and depositing them in the press before they began to ferment. The resulting oil, filtered and decanted, is among those reserved for grand occasions. No one, the olive grower told me, would think of transforming it into soap. Yet that was exactly what I did in the privacy of my room, on an improvised brazier. My experiment was so unsuccessful that I set about varying the formula, using oils of pistachio, bayberry, apricot stones and pine nuts. Two weeks later, I had still made no headway, and exhaustion dogged me. The thirst for vengeance that had first urged me to act now subsided, and I began to question my own obstinacy.

Observing my state of dejection, my friend the glassblower, who by then had managed to sell off all his merchandise and was preparing to return to Hebron, offered to accompany me to the public baths to perk up my spirits. I followed along, feet dragging, to the Hamam al-Shifa, built where Nablus's seven sources of water converge. The structure was crowned with five cupolas of red glass that looked, from the inside, like the cylinders of a kaleidoscope. After exchanging our clothes for a sheet of damask and stepping into wooden clogs, we descended into a hall whose basalt floor was heated by an underground fire. Onto the stone, a hairy satyr threw buckets of water, which immediately evaporated, filling the air with wisps of steam so hellish I could endure no more than a few minutes. In the next room, a young faun with an oiled body beckoned me to lie on an obsidian table and, with a goat's-hair mitt, scrubbed me with the vigor of an animal skinner until my skin turned vermilion. He then suggested an olive-oil rubdown, which I politely declined, as the glassblower had warned me that this particular favor was not one I should accept. We spent the rest of the afternoon in a cooling room where the clients, reclining around a mosaic-lined basin, took tea and savored large squares of sweets made from fine filaments of wheat and sheep's-milk cheese. I closed my eyes and, when I opened them again, dusk had fallen and the hamam was about to close. My friend, who did not want to disturb my sleep, had already left. I quickly dressed and hurried back to the caravansary before nightfall.

Nablus is a city that closes up like a flower at sundown. Bars are dropped across its doors and windows, its market stalls retract, its streets empty. The city takes on an appearance of such uniformity that a person, deprived of his landmarks, quickly becomes disoriented and must search for his path. That is what happened to me. I lost my way in a labyrinth of passageways, each of them identical; I wandered in circles, crossed the same crossroads six times until I finally spotted, as I entered a plaza, a familiar silhouette – that of a chapel located directly behind the caravansary. The chapel housed the remains of Saint Nesta, one of the first martyrs of the early Christian period whose body was discovered intact during exhumation, several centuries after her death. Far be it from me to attack your beliefs, Father, but any soap maker can easily explain such "miracles." It is well known in our profession that, if a coffin is perfectly sealed, a process similar to saponification transforms the fat of the corpse into a whitish substance known as adipocere that protects the flesh from decomposition and exudes a sweet smell associated with saintliness. Be that as it may, a large number of pilgrims had congregated to celebrate the feast of Saint Nesta. They were exiting the church in recessional, each holding votive candles that formed a rosary of light winding across the square. I had no intention of joining their devotions, and was about to push my way between them to reach the street leading to the caravansary, when two words stopped me in my tracks.

Those words – *oleum martyris* – were spoken by a woman who stood apart from the group, and who looked me straight in the eye. Her lips were bloodless and marked by a deep gash that nullified, with one impious stroke, the purity of their line. In the light of the lantern she held close to her face, her skin had the bluish pallor and iridescent glow of opal. Never before, on a living woman, had I seen skin of such color, and I was immediately subjugated. For a moment I believed I was in the presence of a saponified saint! The lady explained to me that the pilgrims had gathered because, each year at this date, the oil of martyrs poured forth from a fissure in the sepulchre of Saint Nesta. The oil, said to be infallible when it came to treating physical and spiritual ills, was collected in a silver vase and siphoned into votive lamps distributed to the faithful. I know I may appear base, but I immediately thought of the soap I could derive from that miraculous oil, and expressed the desire to procure some.

"Don't waste your time," she said. "This deception is nothing more than common olive oil. If you don't believe me, smell it yourself …"

I didn't have to open my nostrils wide to conclude, with cruel disappointment, that she spoke the truth: the air hanging about the chapel was heavy with thick black smoke that stank of rancid frying oil. By contrast, the lady's lamp emitted neither smoke nor smell, and its flame was as transparent as water. Its oil did not exhibit a simple greenish reflection, but an entire prism of iridescences whose forms undulated through the liquid like a mermaid's beckoning dance. When I asked her if it was olive oil, she laughed in my face.

"Your mistake isn't surprising. After all, olive oil enjoys a privileged position in the Church. But there is an oil a thousand times more worthy of being considered holy, for it is of neither vegetable, mineral nor animal origin. This is the oil my lamp burns."

Her words sharpened my desire to acquire it, whatever the price.

"Wait here for me," said the pilgrim. "I will get some for you. And it won't cost you a penny."

I offered to accompany her, but she steadfastly refused, and I let her go her way. But just as I was about to lose sight of her, I began to fear she would slip through my fingers, and decided to follow her at a distance. A slender crescent moon scarcely lit the evening; if I walked slowly, I would not be detected. The lady advanced with the assurance of someone who knows her way, and I followed her without trying to guess where she was leading me. Imagine my surprise when she took me straight to the al-Shifa hamam! Bypassing the main entrance that was tightly padlocked, she slipped through a side door. The lock must have been rusted through, for a sharp blow of her shoulder was enough to force it. By following her, I could have been surprised by a night watchman or fallen into a trap, but those things were far from my mind: the mysterious oil was there, nearby, and I had to have it. It was cool and damp inside the hamam. Without the lamp shining in the distance, I could have been in a tomb. My steps took me into the cooling room where my eyes were drawn to the pool and the sound of lapping water that came from it.

Many are the legends that warn against surprising a woman while she is bathing. The son of a Roman prefect was struck blind by the light shining from the naked body of Saint Agnes. Melusine's husband witnessed her transformation into a serpent. The lecherous elders who observed Susanna were condemned to death. As for wretched Actaeon, guilty of having admired Diana, he was transformed into a stag and torn to pieces by her hounds. When I realized the pilgrim was bathing in the basin, my first reaction was to creep away on tiptoe. But I was discovered before I could take a step.

"So, there you are at last," said the lady, without turning in my direction. "Make yourself useful and pass me the strigil."

Since I did not know the meaning of that word, she pointed to a beveled, bronze-bladed instrument lying by her folded clothes. Before the invention of soap, she told me, the ancients cleaned their skin by scraping it with a strigil, which dislodged the impurities. It is said that the sweat of gladiators thus collected was highly prized by the noble ladies of Rome for its aphrodisiac qualities.

"Like perfume and like wine, oil is extracted by pressure. If you want mine, you'll have to come and get it yourself."

Bronze scraper in hand, I stepped nervously toward the basin. The sense of strangeness grew when I saw that the saponified appearance of her skin extended to her bust. The part of her body under water was hidden by a film of shimmering oil covering the entire surface, and preserving part of her decency.

As if to draw me near, the pilgrim extended her arm. With trembling hand, I drew the strigil down it, from shoulder to wrist. For fear of injuring skin so fine, I hardly pressed on the scraper at all, and so obtained nothing. I had to apply greater force to bring the iridescent sebum from her pores. It had no cause to be jealous of the oil of martyrs and, to gather it, I used the lamp as though it were a chalice. I ran the bronze blade over and over again across her back and hips, following the contours of her belly and her flanks, I slipped under her arms and lingered by her breasts. The strigil granted me liberties my hands would have never taken and I took full advantage, careful not to miss a single drop of holy sebum. I was the mystical press gathering the very essence of a woman – an essence she offered me with a mistress's sense of surrender. I kept the best for last, and could hardly wait to reach the delicious fleshly curves hidden beneath the water's surface. But the pilgrim motioned me to stop.

"If you continue," she said, "you will drain me dry."

I withdrew so that she might get dressed. But when I sought to accompany her, she was no longer in the cooling room. I scoured the hamam, searched the neighboring streets. She had disappeared without a trace. I returned to the caravansary alone and locked myself in my room. I poured the oil from the lamp into a pot and set it over the brazier. There was no need to add ash or glasswort to begin the saponification process; to my astonishment, it occurred spontaneously. The oil lost its transparency and turned cloudy, as white as snow. As it boiled, it threw off so many shimmering bubbles that my room was soon filled with them. Too heavy to float in the air for long, they soon crashed to the floor and burst with a muffled sound. After no more than an hour, the mixture dried and was as hard as a block of marble. It was the perfect bar of soap, complete and without equal. I had produced only one small piece, but enough for me to take revenge and force old al-Jabal to trade his recipe for mine.

The following morning, I put on a clean shirt and prepared myself. As I shaved, I was tempted to try the soap from the mystery woman of the hamam. After all my efforts, didn't I have the right to treat myself to that small luxury? I sliced off a sliver. As soon as it touched my skin, the soap began to lather, though I didn't even need to rub it with water. Its fine and unctuous foam expanded, threatening to overflow my hands. An intimate perfume filled the room, the one women exude in the heat of summer and, I imagine, when they burn with the fires of the night – a perfume with aphrodisiac properties even greater than the sweat of gladiators, to judge by the way it caused my head to spin. I applied the lather to my face and remained for the longest time in its sweetness, amazed that my eyes did not sting at all. Its cleansing property seemed powerful beyond belief, for the lather grew grayer and grayer, like a storm cloud about to burst. With regret, I finally decided to wipe my face. Imagine my dismay when I saw my face was lined with black streaks! I grabbed my razor and tried to scrape away the filth, but it was more tenacious than tar. I could not rinse it off, for water had no effect on the pilgrim's oil that now penetrated my skin. I have always prided myself on my appearance, and could not tolerate looking slovenly. In despair, I went to Jacob's Well, whose water is reputed to have miraculous qualities. The well is located in the crypt of an ancient Orthodox church, guarded by a pope who had to turn the handle a good 140 times to draw the water from the source as many feet below. When at last he handed me the bucket, I felt I was holding a block of ice in my hands. Immediately, I splashed my face. The cursed sebum turned more caustic than an acid bath. I rushed out of the church, howling like a devil in a baptismal font.

Since that misadventure, I can no longer wash my face, for my skin will not tolerate moisture of any kind. The slightest raindrop causes me terrible pain, and my own tears are corrosive. The filth I present to the world is that of the return of the original stain. Only a second baptism can cleanse me of those iniquities, Father, and that is what I have come to ask of you today. I was ready to put Satan, his majesty and all his works behind me. Except that I fear it may be too late. The pilgrim woman has already passed this way. She has profaned the stoups and the baptismal fonts as well. She has replaced the oil in the holy ampullae of the catechumens with her own iridescent sebum; with it she has sullied the altar, the bells and the paten. Can you not smell the loathsome odor that overwhelms even mine? It is human oil that now burns in the sanctuary lamp. Flee, Father. Already she has begun to transform your church into a hellish pandemonium.

OSCULUM INFAME

I SAW YOU MAKE YOUR SIGN of the cross, Father, as I recited the Confiteor. You were staring at the shameful stigma I bear in place of an upper lip, and you feared a creature of the Devil had infiltrated the House of God. Seven men foretold my coming, and warned you against me. They cautioned that I would employ all my evil spells to bring about your ruin. Accustomed as you are to sincere confessions, you did not hesitate to believe them. And now you are trying to catch a glimpse, through the screen, of yellow eyes, waxen skin, snail-shell ears or thorns in my hair ... You are wondering if my spine lengthens into a tail, or if my mons veneris gleams with feathers ...

You are not the first to hear these accusations. They precede me wherever I go to try to escape them; they pursue me relentlessly with all the fury that the gales of calumny can muster. I have endured them until now, and made no effort to refute them. But the time has come for me to defend myself and, at last, bring forth the truth. I pledge not to suppress any part of my own responsibility for the sequence of events that contributed to my downfall. For guilty I am, Father, but in my own way.

It is my fault, my fault, my most grievous fault that I was born to poor parents, too weak to survive an epidemic of typhus. I was twelve years old when they abandoned me to the care of an uncle whom, until then, I never knew. I was driven to his house the day after the burial, and deposited like a bundle of dirty laundry in front of his fine residence on Viger Square. My only baggage was my personal effects, since our creditors had seized what little we possessed. Until then, I did not realize how humble my position was, for my parents, wanting to conceal the inequalities of fortune, had always kept me far from the finer districts. Wealth, for me, consisted of the old, untuned piano in our living room, and the illustrated edition of the *Thousand and One Nights* from which my father would read me a few pages every night.

My uncle was the highly respectable curator of the Museum of Natural Sciences and, walking into his house, I soon became aware of my obscure station. A mute, elderly manservant named Joseph opened the door. His responsibilities were those of majordomo, domestic and cook. He set out down a long corridor, and I followed him into the dining room where my uncle, standing in front of the buffet, was slicing a roast with a well-honed knife. Around the table set with silver and crystal, seven boys waited, the youngest of whom was scarcely older than me. That's how I learned that I had seven cousins. My curiosity about them was not reciprocated: not one of them so much as glanced in my direction. My uncle likewise ignored my presence, and continued slicing the roast with all the concentration of a surgeon. When he had finished distributing the meat, he turned to Joseph and spoke.

"This is the burden that the younger sister of my late wife has deposited on my doorstep. I agreed to take her in, despite the fact that I can suffer no feminine presence in this house. I do not want to see her or hear her. She will take her meals in the kitchen, but will spend the rest of the time in her room, which she is not to leave under any circumstance. May her presence be forgotten, failing which she will find herself in the street again."

I had not expected such a glacial welcome. In silence, I followed Joseph to the basement, and there he showed me a cubbyhole that would be my hiding place. From that day on, I scarcely dared to breathe. Condemned to silence, I listened to the sounds of the house, and tried to distinguish the footsteps. I imagined the comings and goings of each one, and came to know their habits. But soon boredom set in. Without so much as a book to read, what would I do with my days? I began by exploring the basement while old Joseph was out. Then I ventured up to the ground floor while the household slept. I trained myself to make less noise than a mouse; I studied the slats of the parquet, better to avoid those that squeaked. I learned how to slip behind wardrobes, melt into the folds of the draperies, vanish beneath Persian carpets. My gift of invisibility increased each time I emerged from the cubbyhole. Soon, I strolled through the house in broad daylight without attracting attention. More discreet than a shadow, I attended meals in the dining room, listened to the conversations in the living room, watched my cousins play in the attic. The only place that resisted my intrusions was my uncle's office, whose door was always double locked. I was powerfully disappointed; peering through the keyhole, I could see bookshelves crammed with books among which I would have loved to browse at my leisure, especially since, searching through the rest of the house, I had found nothing to read, not even a catechism.

One afternoon, as I was exploring the greenhouse where my uncle cultivated rare crocuses, I came upon a thick volume that had been inadvertently left on a bench. It was a geography textbook into which I quickly delved. The book was illustrated with engravings showing the mosque of Timbuktu, the oasis of al-Hasa, the Zanzibar coast, the churches of Lalibela, the fortress of Muscat, the Damascus caravansary, the bridges of Mosul and other wondrous sites. I was so absorbed in my reading that I forgot about time. Suddenly, a woolen blanket fell over my head and seven pairs of hands grabbed me and threw me to the floor. It was impossible to struggle free; the harder I fought, the tighter the trap shut. I thought I would suffocate, and began to cry. I hadn't shed more than a tear or two, when just as suddenly I was released. When I emerged from the blanket, I saw the crestfallen faces of my seven cousins. It was the first time they were so close, and they seemed quite ugly. Their eyes were pale and protruding, their noses flat, their skin inflamed. Their heads, too heavy for their bodies, wobbled on their skinny necks like the ball atop the spindle of a bilboquet.

"So it *is* true that girls cry," one of them said.

It was Anatole, the eldest. He introduced his brothers: Bastien, Célestin, Désiré, Eugène, François and Gaston, whose alphabetical names I had no difficulty memorizing. I begged them not to turn me over to their father and, since they seemed impressed by tears, I cried all the harder. Célestin asked how much I was ready to pay in exchange for their silence. I knew many tales, and offered to recite one for them. They stared at me, mouths agape.

"What's a tale?" Bastien asked after a lengthy silence.

My cousins had never heard of Perrault, or the *Thousand and One Nights*. My uncle, as befits a naturalist, lectured them on geology, botany and zoology, but found no value in the workings of the imagination. He had chosen to rear his sons in ignorance of music and art, protecting them from the pernicious influence of literature. Why waste time exploring the

imperfect creations of man when one could enjoy the singular privilege of observing the perfect Work of God? I should
have respected my uncle's pedagogical wishes, and pressed no
further. But I was determined to fill the void in my cousins'
education. I invited them to sit and, perched on the bench,
told them the tale of Prince Ahmed. They listened, eyes like
saucers. Once I came to the end, they began picking out the
implausible side of the story.

"Flying carpets do not exist," declared Anatole. "Tomorrow,
try to find a story we can believe."

I asked him if he had a particular subject in mind. He
looked around, then picked a crocus blossom and handed it
to me.

"You can tell us the story of a pistil."

The request surprised me, but I did feel a great sense of
relief: at last I'd found friends with whom I could share, if
only for a few minutes a day. That evening, for the first time
since I'd arrived, I did not mind eating my bowl of gruel alone
in a corner. Lighthearted, I returned to my cubbyhole, since
Anatole had given me permission to secretly borrow the geography textbook. Before going to bed, I read the entire chapter
on Kashmir. The next morning, when I awoke, a tale had taken
shape within me.

My cousins had set our meeting at four o'clock in the garden toolshed. "Our father never goes there," said Célestin. "We
won't need a lookout." I was impatient to meet up with them
and, when the clock struck four, I slipped out the kitchen door.
The shed was hidden behind a bushy hedge of hemlock. It had
long since ceased to house spades, rakes and hoes. My cousins

had transformed it into a clubhouse with stools, and had filled the seed shelves with graduated glass vials like those used by pharmacists. They contained a variety of stagnant, colorless, foamy-looking fluids.

"This is our collection of sputum and saliva!" announced Eugène proudly.

My cousins acquired this viscous assortment by soaking snails and slugs in salt solution, by crushing the heads of garden snakes and toads and wringing the necks of squirrels and birds. They had also accumulated fascinating specimens of spiderwebs and caterpillar cocoons. But the highlight of their collection of slimy curiosities was beyond a doubt seven large jars labeled with each of the boys' names, containing several pints of their spit. Their interest in their phlegm did not end there: every day they organized spitting contests to determine who could spit the farthest and with the greatest accuracy. Anatole, who had ruled the roost for many years, had been recently dethroned by Désiré, who could hit a target ten feet away. My uncle apparently approved, and encouraged the practice with enticing rewards.

"Our father says that's what sets us apart from girls," François explained. "All they do is whine, and they can't even spit."

I couldn't deny that I often cried, and that I found it repugnant to imitate those men who thought nothing of expectorating oyster-sized gobs of spit onto the sidewalk. But I refused to give in when Gaston challenged me to prove the opposite. With aplomb, I took aim at an empty can on the window ledge. Like a pea from a peashooter, a powerful gob of saliva shot from my lips and hit the target so forcefully it toppled over.

"Are you sure you're not a boy?" said François with a whistle of admiration.

I had a hidden talent, I suppose, that I wouldn't have discovered if it hadn't been for my slightly retarded cousins. Still, I was in no hurry to continue the game, and offered to tell them the tale I concocted specifically for them, entitled "The Red Crocus of Srinagar." They liked it so much that they asked me for another, the next day. And that's how we began meeting every day. They would give me a subject, and I would make up a story, using elements from the geography book. There were so many I can't remember all of them: "The Monkey's Tail," "The Grotto of White Insects," "The Yellow Tortoise of Oman," "The Poisoned Prickle," "The Palace of Incense," "The Damascene Fountain Toad," "The Peacock Feather Throne ..." Stories poured from my mouth, as though my saliva gave me words, and all I had to do was spit them out. But eventually the source ran dry. As ill luck would have it, it happened when my cousins asked me for a story about saliva. Try as I might, nothing came to mind. Disconcerted, I asked the boys to give me a few days to think one up. I spent hours in my cubbyhole, poring through the geography textbook without coming upon the slightest idea. A week later, my imagination was still dry. In search of inspiration, I began pacing the hallways. Once more, I found myself in front of my uncle's office door. As I bent to peep through the keyhole, I was utterly surprised to come upon the key that my uncle, in an absentminded act quite unlike him, had forgotten to pocket! The house was empty; I would not be caught. With a trembling hand, I turned the knob and stepped into forbidden territory.

I thought I would find no more than a well-stocked library. Instead, I found myself in a veritable museum. All around me were botanical plates, collections of minerals, insects pinned to felt, skeletons of small mammals mounted in display cases, tortoise shells arranged like armor, bouquets of bird-of-paradise feathers. I never imagined that nature could be so rich in form and color. On the desk, beside an inkwell fashioned from a chambered nautilus fossil, stood a small black pedestal on which rested a strange translucent shell. I drew closer and read the description on the label attached to it.

> *Nidus edulis.* Genus: *Aerodramus.* Species: *fuciphagus.* Made of
> solidified saliva, the nest of the White-nest Swiftlet is a highly
> sought-after dish prized by the emperors of China.

Edible saliva! Another of nature's astonishing miracles. At last I had the subject of my next tale. I was about to leave the room when, in my haste, I knocked over an envelope leaning against the inkwell. I swear, Father, I would never have been so indiscreet as to open it if, when I picked it up, I hadn't noticed the sender's name on the back. The letter was signed in my aunt's handwriting.

The poor woman was not dead, as my uncle claimed, but had been languishing for the last ten years in a padded cell of some asylum where he had her interned. How could I have not been moved as I made out the tormented handwriting of my late mother's sister? The tone of her letter brought tears to my eyes. She begged to be allowed to see her children again; she despaired of ever receiving any news of them; she accused her husband of every cruelty and ended her letter with a litany of imprecations against him. The page was covered with smudges, suggesting my aunt had spat on the paper. I carefully put the envelope back in its place and hurried to join my cousins in the garden toolshed. Mortified, I announced that I had something extremely important to tell them.

"We couldn't care less about your stories," Bastien said disdainfully. "We found out that we can make them up, too. Would you like to hear one?"

I had no choice: I sat down on a stool and opened my ears. Anatole began to speak. His deep voice was soft to the ears, but he clenched his teeth, which gave his tone a hint of malevolence. Instead of telling a story, he revealed that Joseph the manservant was an ex-convict who, before becoming major-domo, had a career as a thief and a con artist. He had robbed the Banque Populaire, been arrested during a shoot-out, then denounced his accomplices to the police to shorten his sentence – an act of betrayal that led to his tongue being cut out in prison.

I interrupted Anatole. I had seen Joseph's tongue, and knew it was perfectly intact. Anatole laughed, and I realized he'd just presented me with a tissue of lies.

"You should be ashamed," I said to him, "defaming poor Joseph who certainly doesn't deserve it."

"You say nasty things in your stories, too," Bastien replied. "What's the difference between your drivel and ours?"

I defended myself. I didn't hurt anyone, since my characters did not exist.

"That's why our stories are more interesting than yours," said Anatole. "And a hundred times better."

"Yes," Désiré chimed in. "And everybody loves to hear them!"

They hadn't kept their nasty gossip to themselves; they had broadcast it through the neighborhood. Joseph was not their only victim. They'd spread the rumor that the schoolmistress still conversed with her dolls, that the dentist constructed pyramids from the teeth he pulled, that the widow Denis powdered her face with plaster of paris, that the old spinsters in the yellow gloves stuffed their mattresses with rubbish gleaned in the park. Of course, these stories were amusing, and you might even smile at them. But most of their gossip was anything but harmless. My cousins claimed that the baker used stray cats as fuel for his oven, that the pharmacist sweetened his wife's tea with arsenic,.that the shoemaker had nailed horseshoes to his daughters' feet to keep them from leaving home, that the vicar recited prayers backward to invoke the powers of Hell. In less than a week, they had irremediably blackened the reputation of honest merchants, generous elders and virtuous mothers.

How could I deny, Father, that I had helped create this infamy? For all my best intentions, my stories acted on them like an evil spell, transforming them into a seven-headed monster, spitting venom on one and all ... I reminded them that bearing false witness is a grave sin, forbidden by the Eighth Commandment; they must make immediate reparation for their acts by reestablishing the truth.

"If your father ever hears of your mischief, I will be the one to be punished."

My cousins found the idea amusing, and they set about devising punishments.

"He will cut off your nose!"

"He will flog you till you bleed!"

"He will starve you!"

"He will make you crawl before him!"

"He will burn out your eyes!"

"He will throw you into the brambles!"

"He will rub your face in the mud!"

None of those possibilities impressed me unduly.

"I know better than you what awaits me," I told them. "He will have me locked up in the same asylum where your poor mother has been languishing for ten years!"

I owe all my sufferings, Father, to those unfortunate words, for no sooner had I spoken them than my cousins turned their hateful gaze on me. I had thought they would have rejoiced to learn their mother was still alive, that they would have been grateful for the revelation. But they refused to accept the possibility. They preferred to think she was dead than picture her in an insane asylum, and they could not imagine that their father had been lying to them all these years. The more I insisted I was telling the truth, and that I had proof of what I was saying, the more they accused me of being the most vile liar who ever walked the face of the earth.

"You have dared to dishonor the memory of our saintly mother."

"You have born false witness against our father, who took you in with open arms."

"You have mocked our pain."

"You have exceeded the bounds of treachery."

"You will soon have to answer for what you said."

～

The time of vengeance was not long in coming. One Sunday afternoon, Gaston knocked on the door of my cubbyhole and told me to follow him.

"Quick," he insisted. "We've just made a major scientific discovery."

For me, the news came as a relief. If my cousins had resumed their experiments, perhaps that meant they had stopped spreading gossip. I went to the dining room with Gaston. At the threshold, I hung back, for it was almost time for dinner, and my uncle would soon appear. François assured me that the demonstration would be brief, and he pulled me by my sleeve to the table, which was already set. The crystal glasses were filled with milky liquid. Eugène picked one up and held it under my nose.

"Do you want a taste?"

The odor was not very appealing: a mixture of bleach and curdled cream. I pushed the glass away in disgust.

"From what new animal have you extracted this slime?"

Anatole put on an insulted expression.

"Don't you know anything about saliva? We've discovered a new way of spitting."

I knew almost nothing about the nature of boys of that age. But when I saw my cousins unbutton their trousers and jiggle their hands in their pants, I knew immediately they were up to no good. I asked them to stop that ridiculous activity, but they would not listen. Then, in unison, each one of them shot a gob of white spit into his glass. I was so shocked I started to scream. Just then the dining-room door swung open loudly.

My uncle did not deign to look at me, no more then than the first day.

"How did she get in here?" he asked his sons.

Anatole stepped forward with an accusing finger and declared I was rabid.

"We caught her running around the table in circles. She was foaming at the mouth and spitting in our glasses."

How can you defend yourself against false witness, Father? On my knees, I pleaded with my uncle to grant me a fair hearing, and listen to my version of the facts. I hid nothing of the ignominy to which his sons had exposed themselves. When he ordered them to take their places at the table, I thought I had finally succeeded in convincing him of my innocence.

"Never in my life," he said to them, "have I heard such outrageous utterances!"

But instead of punishing the guilty, he picked up his large carving knife and stepped toward me. He grabbed me by the hair to hold my head still, then slipped the long blade across my upper lip, bearing down to slice through the flesh.

"I bestow upon you the *osculum infame*," he proclaimed in solemn tones. "The kiss of shame. The one the Devil uses to seal his alliances. From now forward, all will know that behind this cleft lip hides a forked tongue. No one will ever listen to your lies again."

I tried to stanch the blood that flowed down my chin, but he prevented me.

"First, you will taste your venom."

He paraded my cousins before me with their spit-filled glasses. One by one, they held them to my lips. I was forced to swallow their contents to the last drop.

≈

That, Father, was only the beginning of my suffering. I will not subject you to the story of what I had to endure in that house of torture. Even a hardened soul such as yours would find it intolerable. It is enough for you to know that, when I finally managed to escape, I fled to the ends of the earth. But that was not far enough. In the heights of Kashmir, in farthest Persia, in the depths of Yemen, my cousins sought me out. They hunted me down, and each time inflicted new torments upon me. Not content merely to disfigure me, they made me invisible. They reduced me to silence. They confiscated my name. Even after they made me disappear, they continued their work. They dishonored me. They stripped me of all credibility. Because of them, people looked askance at me, insulted me, slammed doors in my face. I lived like an exile, never knowing the sweetness of hearth and home. I was forced to give up on friendship, love, life itself.

They did not have the courage to confess their darkest crimes to you. They disguised them behind fables in which they assume the victim's role. And you, a voyeur of the ear, you listened to them with malignant curiosity. You encouraged them to recite their shameless lies, pour out their false affirmations, conceal their malevolent intentions. You went so far as to give them absolution, allowing the sacrament of confession to become impure mystification! And when I came to you in all good faith, you feared me. You crossed yourself and muttered, "*Vade retro, Satana!*" Even before I could speak a single word in my defense, you declared yourself a divine judge and made this confessional the supreme tribunal. You were ready to excommunicate me, and condemn me to eternal damnation. Father, you were not entirely wrong.

Since you have taken an oath to observe the silence of the grave, I can confess everything to you. I have committed the gravest of sins. But I can whisper my peccavi only in the lowest of voices. If you wish to hear it, you must draw nearer. Come closer. Closer still. Press your ear against the screen as I have pressed my lips, and open wide. I admit: there is an element of truth in what my cousins have told you. My hatred of them has transformed me. I am no longer a woman. I am a demon of vengeance, the sum of their calumnies, and on my body I bear diabolical remnants. With my skin, my tail, my thorns, I have cursed my torturers. That is the truth, Father. I swear on this spit.

No use reaching for your handkerchief. The hot, viscous venom that passed through the screen has already reached your auricle. It does not heal like the saliva of Christ. It is more corrosive than acid. Can you feel it burning through your eardrum? It will travel deep into the seat of your hearing. I would have preferred to spit in God's face, He who remained so stubbornly deaf to my prayers. But I will have to settle for sullying His ear on earth. Console yourself, Father; you will not have to listen to any more lies. With my saliva, I have sealed off the gates of malicious gossip. This is the last confession you will hear. Perhaps you will find serenity in the silence that will soon surround you. Are you having trouble understanding my words? My voice is becoming more and more distant … In any event, I have said enough.

Farewell. Go in peace.

ACKNOWLEDGMENTS

To David Homel and Fred A. Reed, my faithful and loyal translators, as well as Kevin Williams and everyone at Talonbooks.

To the tireless Antoine Tanguay, the spark of the twenty-fifth hour; for the flawless Julie Robert and the wonderful team at Alto: Patricia Lamy, Robert Tanguay, Dominique Fortier, Louis Gagné and Isabelle Tousignant.

To my first readers: my beloved goddaughter Gabrielle Martin, Pierre Filion, Gilles Jobidon, Isabelle Grégoire, Ingeborg Reed, Sophie Cardinal-Corriveau and André Ducharme, for their enthusiasm and indulgence.

To the team at *L'actualité*: Ginette Haché, Carole Beaulieu, Chantale Cusson, Pierre Cayouette, Lucie Daigle, Julie Duguay, Ginette Dupuis, Louise Gendron, Marie-Laure Godefroy and Charles Grandmont, for their support and encouragement.

To all those who, sporadically, were kind enough to inquire about the progress of this book: Dominique Drouin, Marc Gamelin, Nicolas Martin, Rod Mickleburgh, Jim Firstbrook, Jean-Philippe Chénier, Ihosvany Hernández Gonzáles, Louis Duhamel, Nathan Dratler, Frédéric Boileau, Line Lafontaine, Luigi Delle Donne, Michel Héroux, Jean Lamarre, Beaudoin Daigneault, Michel Chioini, Frank McLaughlin and Claude Pinsonnault.

To my unfailing siblings Lucie, Louis, Élise, Michèle and Mireille, and to my parents.

To Winnie the fox terrier, for her joyful companionship.

And especially, as always, infinitely, to Serge.

A three-time winner of the Governor General's Award for translation, plus a nomination in 2009 for his translation of Thierry Hentsch's *Le temps aboli, Empire of Desire,* **Fred A. Reed** has translated works by many of Quebec's leading authors, several in collaboration with novelist David Homel, as well as by Nikos Kazantzakis and other modern Greek writers. Reed worked with documentarist Jean-Daniel Lafond on two documentary films: *Salam Iran: A Persian Letter* and *American Fugitive.* The two later collaborated on *Conversations in Tehran* (Talonbooks, 2006). His latest work is *Then We Were One,* published in 2011 by Talonbooks. Fred A. Reed resides in Montreal.

Award-winning novelist and literary translator **David Homel** also works as a journalist, editor, and screenwriter. He was born in Chicago in 1952 but left at the end of the tumultuous 1960s to continue his education in Europe and Toronto before settling in Montreal in around 1980. He worked at a variety of industrial jobs before beginning to write fiction in the mid-1980s. His nine novels to date have been translated into several languages and published around the world.

Martine Desjardins was born in the Town of Mount Royal in Quebec in 1957. The second child of six, she started writing short stories when she was seventeen. After receiving a bachelor's degree in Russian and Italian studies at the University of Montreal, she went on to complete a master's degree in comparative literature, exploring humor in Dostoevsky's *The Devils*. She worked as an assistant editor-in-chief at *ELLE Québec* magazine for four years before leaving to devote herself to writing. Presently she works as a freelance rewriter, translator and journalist for *L'actualité*, an award-winning French-language current affairs magazine in Canada. Her first novel, *Le cercle de Clara*, was published by Leméac in 1997, and was nominated for both the Prix littéraires du Québec and the Grand Prix des lectrices de ELLE Québec in 1998. It has been published by Talonbooks in English as *Fairy Ring*. *Maleficium* was published in 2009 by Éditions Alto, won the Prix Jacques-Brossard and was a finalist for the Prix des libraires du Québec in 2010, the Prix des cinq continents de la Francophonie and the Prix France–Québec. Desjardins currently lives in the Town of Mount Royal with her husband. In her free time, she paints miniature models of ruins overgrown with vegetation.